Knights of the Art: Stories

Amy Steedman

Table of Contents

Knights of the Art: Stories..1

Amy Steedman...1

ABOUT THIS BOOK...1

FRA ANGELICO...11

MASACCIO..15

FRA FILIPPO LIPPI...17

SANDRO BOTTICELLI...37

DOMENICO GHIRLANDAIO..44

FILIPPINO LIPPI..50

PIETRO PERUGINO...53

LEONARDO DA VINCI..64

RAPHAEL..77

MICHELANGELO...81

ANDREA DEL SARTO...88

GIOVANNI BELLINI..95

GIORGIONE..102

TITIAN...107

PAUL VERONESE...113

Knights of the Art: Stories

Amy Steedman

TO FRANCESCA

ABOUT THIS BOOK

What would we do without our picture−books, I wonder? Before we knew how to read, before even we could speak, we had learned to love them. We shouted with pleasure when we turned the pages and saw the spotted cow standing in the daisy− sprinkled meadow, the foolish−looking old sheep with her gambolling lambs, the wise dog with his friendly eyes. They were all real friends to us.

Then a little later on, when we began to ask for stories about the pictures, how we loved them more and more. There was the little girl in the red cloak talking to the great grey wolf with the wicked eyes; the cottage with the bright pink roses climbing round the lattice−window, out of which jumped a little maid with golden hair, followed by the great big bear, the middle−sized bear, and the tiny bear. Truly those stories were a great joy to us, but we would never have loved them quite so much if we had not known their pictured faces as well.

Do you ever wonder how all these pictures came to be made? They had a beginning, just as everything else had, but the beginning goes so far back that we can scarcely trace it.

Children have not always had picture−books to look at. In the long−ago days such things were not known. Thousands of years ago, far away in Assyria, the Assyrian people learned to make pictures and to carve them out in stone. In Egypt, too, the Egyptians traced pictures upon the walls of their temples and upon the painted mummy− cases of the dead. Then the Greeks made still more beautiful statues and pictures in marble, and called them gods and goddesses, for all this was at a time when the true God was forgotten.

Afterwards, when Christ had come and the people had learned that the pictured gods were not real, they began to think it wicked to make beautiful pictures or carve marble statues. The few pictures that were made were stiff and ugly, the figures were not like real men and women, the animals and trees were very strange–looking things. And instead of making the sky blue as it really was, they made it a chequered pattern of gold. After a time it seemed as if the art of making pictures was going to die out altogether.

Then came the time which is called `The Renaissance,' a word which means being born again, or a new awakening, when men began to draw real pictures of real things and fill the world with images of beauty.

Now it is the stories of the men of that time, who put new life into Art, that I am going to tell you— men who learned, step by step, to paint the most beautiful pictures that the world possesses.

In telling these stories I have been helped by an old book called The Lives of the Painters, by Giorgio Vasari, who was himself a painter. He took great delight in gathering together all the stories about these artists and writing them down with loving care, so that he shows us real living men, and not merely great names by which the famous pictures are known.

It did not make much difference to us when we were little children whether our pictures were good or bad, as long as the colours were bright and we knew what they meant. But as we grow older and wiser our eyes grow wiser too, and we learn to know what is good and what is poor. Only, just as our tongues must be trained to speak, our hands to work, and our ears to love good music, so our eyes must be taught to see what is beautiful, or we may perhaps pass it carelessly by, and lose a great joy which might be ours.

So now if you learn something about these great artists and their wonderful pictures, it will help your eyes to grow wise. And some day should you visit sunny Italy, where these men lived and worked, you will feel that they are quite old friends. Their pictures will not only be a delight to your eyes, but will teach your heart something deeper and more wonderful than any words can explain. AMY STEEDMAN

```
GIOTTO, . . . BORN 1276,      DIED 1337
FRA ANGELICO, . . " 1387,       " 1466
MASACCIO, . . . " 1401,       " 1428
FRA FILIPPO LIPPI,. . " 1412,      " 1469
SANDRO BOTTICELLI,. . " 1446,       " 1610
DOMENICO GHIRLANDAIO, " 1449,        " 1494
FILIPPINO LIP . . " 1467,       " 1604
PIETRO PERUGINO, . " 1446,        " 1624
LEONARDO DA VINCI,. . " 1462,        " 1619
RAPHAEL, . . . " 1483,       " 1620
MICHELANGELO, . . " 1476,       " 1664
ANDREA DEL SARTO, . " 1487,       " 1631
GIOVANNI BELLINI, . " 1426,       " 1616
VITTORE CARPACCIO,. . " 1470?       " 1619
GIORGIONE, . . " 1477?       " 1610
TITIAN, . . . " 1477,       " 1676
TINTORETTO, . . " 1662,       " 1637
PAUL VERONESE,. . " 1628,       " 1688
```

GIOTTO

It was more than six hundred years ago that a little peasant baby was born in the small village of Vespignano, not far from the beautiful city of Florence, in Italy. The baby's father, an honest, hard–working countryman, was called Bondone, and the name he gave to his little son was Giotto.

Life was rough and hard in that country home, but the peasant baby grew into a strong, hardy boy, learning early what cold and hunger meant. The hills which surrounded the village were grey and bare, save where the silver of the olive–trees shone in the sunlight, or the tender green of the shooting corn made the valley beautiful in early spring. In summer there was little shade from the blazing sun as it rode high in the blue sky, and the grass which grew among the grey rocks was often burnt and brown. But, nevertheless, it was here that the sheep of the village would be turned out to find what food they could, tended and watched by one of the village boys.

So it happened that when Giotto was ten years old his father sent him to take care of the sheep upon the hillside. Country boys had then no schools to go to or lessons to learn, and Giotto spent long happy days, in sunshine and rain, as he followed the sheep from place to place, wherever they could find grass enough to feed on. But Giotto did something else besides watching his sheep. Indeed, he sometimes forgot all about them, and many a search he had to gather them all together again. For there was one thing he loved doing better than all beside, and that was to try to draw pictures of all the things he saw around him.

It was no easy matter for the little shepherd lad. He had no pencils or paper, and he had never, perhaps, seen a picture in all his life. But all this mattered little to him. Out there, under the blue sky, his eyes made pictures for him out of the fleecy white clouds as they slowly changed from one form to another. He learned to know exactly the shape of every flower and how it grew; he noticed how the olive–trees laid their silver leaves against the blue background of the sky that peeped in between, and how his sheep looked as they stooped to eat, or lay down in the shadow of a rock.

Nothing escaped his keen, watchful eyes, and then with eager hands he would sharpen a piece of stone, choose out the smoothest rock, and try to draw on its flat surface all those wonderful shapes which had filled his eyes with their beauty. Olive–trees, flowers, birds and beasts were there, but especially his sheep, for they were his friends and companions who were always near him, and he could draw them in a different way each time they moved.

Now it fell out that one day a great master painter from Florence came riding through the valley and over the hills where Giotto was feeding his sheep. The name of the great master was Cimabue, and he was the most wonderful artist in the world, so men said. He had painted a picture which had made all Florence rejoice. The Florentines had never seen anything like it before, and yet it was but a strange– looking portrait of the Madonna and Child, scarcely like a real woman or a real baby at all. Still, it seemed to them a perfect wonder, and Cimabue was honoured as one of the city's greatest men.

The road was lonely as it wound along. There was nothing to be seen but waves of grey hills on every side, so the stranger rode on, scarcely lifting his eyes as he went. Then suddenly he came upon a flock of sheep nibbling the scanty sunburnt grass, and a little brown–faced shepherd–boy gave him a cheerful `Good–day, master.'

There was something so bright and merry in the boy's smile that the great man stopped and began to talk to him. Then his eye fell upon the smooth flat rock over which the boy had been bending, and he started with surprise.

`Who did that?' he asked quickly, and he pointed to the outline of a sheep scratched upon the stone.

`It is the picture of one of my sheep there,' answered the boy, hanging his head with a shame– faced look. `I drew it with this,' and he held out towards the stranger the sharp stone he had been using.

`Who taught you to do this?' asked the master as he looked more carefully at the lines drawn on the rock.

The boy opened his eyes wide with astonishment `Nobody taught me, master,' he said. `I only try to draw the things that my eyes see.'

`How would you like to come with me to Florence and learn to be a painter?' asked Cimabue, for he saw that the boy had a wonderful power in his little rough hands.

Giotto's cheeks flushed, and his eyes shone with joy.

`Indeed, master, I would come most willingly,' he cried, `if only my father will allow it.'

So back they went together to the village, but not before Giotto had carefully put his sheep into the fold, for he was never one to leave his work half done.

Bondone was amazed to see his boy in company with such a grand stranger, but he was still more surprised when he heard of the stranger's offer. It seemed a golden chance, and he gladly gave his consent.

Why, of course, the boy should go to Florence if the gracious master would take him and teach him to become a painter. The home would be lonely without the boy who was so full of fun and as bright as a sunbeam. But such chances were not to be met with every day, and he was more than willing to let him go.

So the master set out, and the boy Giotto went with him to Florence to begin his training.

The studio where Cimabue worked was not at all like those artists' rooms which we now call studios. It was much more like a workshop, and the boys who went there to learn how to draw and paint were taught first how to grind and prepare the colours and then to mix them. They were not allowed to touch a brush or pencil for a long time, but only to watch their master at work, and learn all that they could from what they saw him do.

So there the boy Giotto worked and watched, but when his turn came to use the brush, to the amazement of all, his pictures were quite unlike anything which had ever been painted before in the workshop. Instead of copying the stiff, unreal figures, he drew real people, real animals, and all the things which he had learned to know so well on the grey hillside, when he watched his father's sheep. Other artists had painted the Madonna and Infant Christ, but Giotto painted a mother and a baby.

And before long this worked such a wonderful change that it seemed indeed as if the art of making pictures had been born again. To us his work still looks stiff and strange, but in it was the beginning of all the beautiful pictures that belong to us now.

Giotto did not only paint pictures, he worked in marble as well. To–day, if you walk through Florence, the City of Flowers, you will still see its fairest flower of all, the tall white campanile or bell– tower, `Giotto's tower' as it is called. There it stands in all its grace and loveliness like a tall white lily against the blue sky, pointing ever upward, in the grand old faith of the shepherd–boy. Day after day it calls to prayer and to good works, as it has done all these hundreds of years since Giotto designed and helped to build it.

Some people call his pictures stiff and ugly, for not every one has wise eyes to see their beauty, but the loveliness of this tower can easily be seen by all. `There the white doves circle round and round, and rest in the sheltering niches of the delicately carved arches; there at the call of its bell the black–robed Brothers of Pity hurry past to their works of mercy. There too the little children play, and sometimes stop to stare at the marble pictures, set in the first story of the tower, low enough to be seen from the street. Their special favourite is perhaps the picture of the shepherd sitting under his tent, with the sheep in front, and with the funniest little dog keeping watch at the side.

Giotto always had a great love for animals, and whenever it was possible he would squeeze one into a corner of his pictures. He was sixty years old when he designed this wonderful tower and cut some of the marble pictures with his own hand, but you can see that the memory of those old days when he ran barefoot about the hills and tended his sheep was with him still. Just such another little puppy must have often played with him in those long–ago days before he became a great painter and was still only a merry, brown–faced boy, making pictures with a sharp stone upon the smooth rocks.

Up and down the narrow streets of Florence now, the great painter would walk and watch the faces of the people as they passed. And his eyes would still make pictures of them and their busy life, just as they used to do with the olive–trees, the sheep, and the clouds.

In those days nobody cared to have pictures in their houses, and only the walls of the churches were painted. So the pictures, or frescoes, as they were called, were of course all about sacred subjects, either stories out of the Bible or of the lives of the saints. And as there were few books, and the poor people did not know how to read, these frescoed walls were the only story–books they had.

What a joy those pictures of Giotto's must have been, then, to those poor folk! They looked at the little Baby Jesus sitting on His mother's knee, wrapped in swaddling bands, just like one of their own little ones, and it made Him seem a very real baby. The wise men who talked together and pointed to the shining star overhead looked just like any of the great nobles of Florence. And there at the back were the two horses looking on with wise interested eyes, just as any of their own horses might have done.

It seemed to make the story of Christmas a thing which had really happened, instead of a far–away tale which had little meaning for them. Heaven and the Madonna were not so far off after all. And it comforted them to think that the Madonna had been a real woman like themselves, and that the Jesu Bambino would stoop to bless them still, just as He leaned forward to bless the wise men in the picture.

How real too would seem the old story of the meeting of Anna and Joachim at the Golden Gate, when they could gaze upon the two homely figures under the narrow gateway. No visionary saints these, but just a simple husband and wife, meeting each other with joy after a sad separation, and yet with the touch of heavenly meaning shown by the angel who hovers above and places a hand upon each head.

It was not only in Florence that Giotto did his work. His fame spread far and wide, and he went from town to town eagerly welcomed by all. We can trace his footsteps as he went, by those wonderful old pictures which he spread with loving care over the bare walls of the churches, lifting, as it were, the curtain that hides Heaven from our view and bringing some of its joys to earth.

Then, at Assisi, he covered the walls and ceiling of the church with the wonderful frescoes of the life of St. Francis; and the little round commonplace Arena Chapel of Padua is made exquisite inside by his pictures of the life of our Lord.

In the days when Giotto lived the towns of Italy were continually quarrelling with one another, and there was always fighting going on somewhere. The cities were built with a wall all round them, and the gates were shut each night to keep out their enemies. But often the fighting was between different families inside the city, and the grim old palaces in the narrow streets were built tall and strong that they might be the more easily defended.

In the midst of all this war and quarrelling Giotto lived his quiet, peaceful life, the friend of every one and the enemy of none. Rival towns sent for him to paint their churches with his heavenly pictures, and the people who hated Florence forgot that he was a Florentine. He was just Giotto, and he belonged to them all. His brush was the white flag of truce which made men forget their strife and angry passions, and turned their thoughts to holier things.

Even the great poet Dante did not scorn to be a friend of the peasant painter, and we still have the portrait which Giotto painted of him in an old fresco at Florence. Later on, when the great poet was a poor unhappy exile, Giotto met him again at Padua and helped to cheer some of those sad grey days, made so bitter by strife and injustice.

Now when Giotto was beginning to grow famous, it happened that the Pope was anxious to have the walls of the great Cathedral of St. Peter at Rome decorated. So he sent messengers all over Italy to find out who were the best painters, that he might invite them to come and do the work.

The messengers went from town to town and asked every artist for a specimen of his painting. This was gladly given, for it was counted a great honour to help to make St.

Peter's beautiful.

By and by the messengers came to Giotto and told him their errand. The Pope, they said, wished to see one of his drawings to judge if he was fit for the great work. Giotto, who was always most courteous, `took a sheet of paper and a pencil dipped in a red colour, then, resting his elbow on his side, with one turn of the hand, he drew a circle so perfect and exact that it was a marvel to behold.' `Here is your drawing,' he said to the messenger, with a smile, handing him the drawing.

`Am I to have nothing more than this?' asked the man, staring at the red circle in astonishment and disgust.

`That is enough and to spare,' answered Giotto. `Send it with the rest.'

The messengers thought this must all be a joke.

`How foolish we shall look if we take only a round O to show his Holiness,' they said.

But they could get nothing else from Giotto, so they were obliged to be content and to send it with the other drawings, taking care to explain just how it was done.

The Pope and his advisers looked carefully over all the drawings, and, when they came to that round O, they knew that only a master–hand could have made such a perfect circle without the help of a compass. Without a moment's hesitation they decided that Giotto was the man they wanted, and they at once invited him to come to Rome to decorate the cathedral walls. So when the story was known the people became prouder than ever of their great painter, and the round O of Giotto has become a proverb to this day in Tuscany.

`Round as the O of Giotto, d' ye see; Which means as well done as a thing can be.'

Later on, when Giotto was at Naples, he was painting in the palace chapel one very hot day, when the king came in to watch him at his work. It really was almost too hot to move, and yet Giotto painted away busily.

`Giotto,' said the king, `if I were in thy place I would give up painting for a while and take my rest, now that it is so hot.'

`And, indeed, so I would most certainly do,' answered Giotto, `if I were in your place, your Majesty.'

It was these quick answers and his merry smile that charmed every one, and made the painter a favourite with rich and poor alike.

There are a great many stories told of him, and they all show what a sunny–tempered, kindly man he was.

It is said that one day he was standing in one of the narrow streets of Florence talking very earnestly to a friend, when a pig came running down the road in a great hurry. It did not stop to look where it was going, but ran right between the painter's legs and knocked him flat on his back, putting an end to his learned talk.

Giotto scrambled to his feet with a rueful smile, and shook his finger at the pig which was fast disappearing in the distance.

`Ah, well!' he said, `I suppose thou hadst as much right to the road as I had. Besides, how many gold pieces I have earned by the help of thy bristles, and never have I given any of thy family even a drop of soup in payment.'

Another time he went riding with a very learned lawyer into the country to look after his property. For when Bondone died, he left all his fields and his farm to his painter son. Very soon a storm came on, and the rain poured down as if it never meant to stop.

`Let us seek shelter in this farmhouse and borrow a cloak,' suggested Giotto.

So they went in and borrowed two old cloaks from the farmer, and wrapped themselves up from head to foot. Then they mounted their horses and rode back together to Florence.

Presently the lawyer turned to look at Giotto, and immediately burst into a loud laugh. The rain was running from the painter's cap, he was splashed with mud, and the old cloak made him look like a very forlorn beggar.

`Dost think if any one met thee now, they would believe that thou art the best painter in the world?' laughed the lawyer.

Giotto's eyes twinkled as he looked at the funny figure riding beside him, for the lawyer was very small, and had a crooked back, and rolled up in the old cloak he looked like a bundle of rags.

`Yes!' he answered quickly, `any one would certainly believe I was a great painter, if he could but first persuade himself that thou dost know thy A B C.'

In all these stories we catch glimpses of the good–natured kindly painter, with his love of jokes, and his own ready answers, and all the time we must remember that he was filling the world with beauty, which it still treasures to–day, helping to sow the seeds of that great tree of Art which was to blossom so gloriously in later years.

And when he had finished his earthly work it was in his own cathedral, `St. Mary of the Flowers,' that they laid him to rest, while the people mourned him as a good friend as well as a great painter. There he lies in the shadow of his lily tower, whose slender grace and delicate–tinted marbles keep his memory ever fresh in his beautiful city of Florence.

FRA ANGELICO

Nearly a hundred years had passed by since Giotto lived and worked in Florence, and in the same hilly country where he used to tend his sheep another great painter was born.

Many other artists had come and gone, and had added their golden links of beauty to the chain of Art which bound these years together. Some day you will learn to know all their names and what they did. But now we will only single out, here and there, a few of those names which are perhaps greater than the rest. Just as on a clear night, when we look up into the starlit sky, it would bewilder us to try and remember all the stars, so we learn first to know those that are most easily recognised—the Plough, or the Great Bear, as they shine with a clear steady light against the background of a thousand lesser stars.

The name by which this second great painter is known is Fra Angelico, but that was only the name he earned in later years. His baby name was Guido, and his home was in a village close to where Giotto was born.

He was not a poor boy, and did not need to work in the fields or tend the sheep on the hillside. Indeed, he might have soon become rich and famous, for his wonderful talent for painting would have quickly brought him honours and wealth if he had gone out into the world. But instead of this, when he was a young man of twenty he made up his mind to enter the convent at Fiesole, and to become a monk of the Order of Saint Dominic.

Every brother, or frate, as he is called, who leaves the world and enters the life of the convent is given a new name, and his old name is never used again. So young Guido was called Fra Giovanni, or Brother John. But it is not by that name that he is known best, but that of Fra Angelico, or the angelic brother—a name which was given him afterwards because of his pure and beautiful life, and the heavenly pictures which he painted.

With all his great gifts in his hands, with all the years of youth and pleasure stretching out green and fair before him, he said good–bye to earthly joys, and chose rather to serve his Master Christ in the way he thought was right.

The monks of St. Dominic were the great preachers of those days—men who tried to make the world better by telling people what they ought to do, and teaching them how to live honest and good lives. But there are other ways of teaching people besides preaching, and the young monk who spent his time bending over the illuminated prayer- book, seeing with his dreamy eyes visions of saints and white–robed angels, was preparing to be a greater teacher than them all. The words of the preacher monks have passed away, and the world pays little heed to them now, but the teaching of Fra Angelico, the silent lessons of his wonderful pictures, are as fresh and clear to–day as they were in those far–off years.

Great trouble was in store for the monks of the little convent at Fiesole, which Fra Angelico and his brother Benedetto had entered. Fierce struggles were going on in Italy between different religious parties, and at one time the little band of preaching monks were obliged to leave their peaceful home at Fiesole to seek shelter in other towns. But, as it turned out, this was good fortune for the young painter–monk, for in those hill towns of Umbria where the brothers sought refuge there were pictures to be studied which delighted his eyes with their beauty, and taught him many a lesson which he could never have learned on the quiet slopes of Fiesole.

Knights of the Art: Stories

The hill towns of Italy are very much the same to–day as they were in those days. Long winding roads lead upwards from the plain below to the city gates, and there on the summit of the hill the little town is built. The tall white houses cluster close together, and the overhanging eaves seem almost to meet across the narrow paved streets, and always there is the great square, with the church the centre of all.

It would be almost a day's journey to follow the white road that leads down from Perugia across the plain to the little hill town of Assisi, and many a spring morning saw the painter–monk setting out on the convent donkey before sunrise and returning when the sun had set. He would thread his way up between the olive–trees until he reached the city gates, and pass into the little town without hindrance. For the followers of St. Francis in their brown robes would be glad to welcome a stranger monk, though his black robe showed that he belonged to a different order. Any one who came to see the glory of their city, the church where their saint lay, which Giotto had covered with his wonderful pictures, was never refused admittance.

How often then must Fra Angelico have knelt in the dim light of that lower church of Assisi, learning his lesson on his knees, as was ever his habit. Then home again he would wend his way, his eyes filled with visions of those beautiful pictures, and his hand longing for the pencil and brush, that he might add new beauty to his own work from what he had learned.

Several years passed by, and at last the brothers were allowed to return to their convent home of San Dominico at Fiesole, and there they lived peaceably for a long time. We cannot tell exactly what pictures our painter–monk painted during those peaceful years, but we know he must have been looking out with wise, seeing eyes, drinking in all the beauty that was spread around him.

At his feet lay Florence, with its towers and palaces, the Arno running through it like a silver thread, and beyond, the purple of the Tuscan hills. All around on the sheltered hillside were green vines and fruit–trees, olives and cypresses, fields flaming in spring with scarlet anemones or golden with great yellow tulips, and hedges of rose–bushes covered with clusters of pink blossoms. No wonder, then, such beauty sunk into his heart, and we see in his pictures the pure fresh colour of the spring flowers, with no shadow of dark or evil things.

Soon the fame of the painter began to be whispered outside the convent walls, and reached the ears of Cosimo da Medici, one of the powerful rulers of Florence. He offered the monks a new home, and, when they were settled in the convent of San Marco in Florence, he invited Fra Angelico to fresco the walls.

One by one the heavenly pictures were painted upon the walls of the cells and cloister of the new home. How the brothers must have crowded round to see each new fresco as it was finished, and how anxious they would be to see which picture was to be near their own particular bed. In all the frescoes, whether he painted the gentle Virgin bending before the angel messenger, or tried to show the glory of the ascended Lord, the artist–monk would always introduce one or more of the convent's special saints, which made the brothers feel that the pictures were their very own. Fra Angelico had a kind word and smile for all the brothers. He was never impatient, and no one ever saw him angry, for he was as humble and gentle as the saints whose pictures he loved to paint.

It is told of him, too, that he never took a brush or pencil in his hand without a prayer that his work might be to the glory of God. Often when he painted the sufferings of our Lord, the tears would be seen running down his cheeks and almost blinding his eyes.

There is an old legend which tells of a certain monk who, when he was busily illuminating a page of his missal, was called away to do some service for the poor. He went unwillingly, the legend says, for he longed to put the last touches to the holy picture he was painting; but when he returned, lo! he found his work finished by angel hands.

Often when we look at some of Fra Angelico's pictures we are reminded of this legend, and feel that he too might have been helped by those same angel hands. Did they indeed touch his eyes that he might catch glimpses of a Heaven where saints were swinging their golden censers, and white–robed angels danced in the flowery meadows of Paradise? We cannot tell; but this we know, that no other painter has ever shown us such a glory of heavenly things.

Best of all, the angel–painter loved to paint pictures of the life of our Lord; and in the picture I have shown you, you will see the tender care with which he has drawn the head of the Infant Jesus with His little golden halo, the Madonna in her robe of purest blue, holding the Baby close in her arms, St. Joseph the guardian walking at the side, and all around the flowers and trees which he loved so well in the quiet home of Fiesole.

He did not care for fame or power, this dreamy painter of angels, and when the Pope invited him to Rome to paint the walls of a chapel there, he thought no more of the glory and honour than if he was but called upon to paint another cell at San Marco.

But when the Pope had seen what this quiet monk could do, he called the artist to him.

`A man who can paint such pictures,' he said, `must be a good man, and one who will do well whatever he undertakes. Will you, then, do other work for me, and become my Archbishop at Florence?' But the painter was startled and dismayed.

`I cannot teach or preach or govern men,' he said, `I can but use my gift of painting for the glory of God. Let me rather be as I am, for it is safer to obey than to rule.'

But though he would not take this honour himself, he told the Pope of a friend of his, a humble brother, Fra Antonino, at the convent of San Marco, who was well fitted to do the work. So the Pope took the painter's advice, and the choice was so wise and good, that to this day the Florentine people talk lovingly of their good bishop Antonino.

It was while he was at work in Rome that Fra Angelico died, so his body does not rest in his own beloved Florence. But if his body lies in Rome, his gentle spirit still seems to hover around the old convent of San Marco, and there we learn to know and love him best. Little wonder that in after ages they looked upon him almost as a saint, and gave him the title of `Beato,' or the blessed angel– painter.

MASACCIO

It must have been about the same time when Fra Angelico was covering the walls of San Marco with his angel pictures, that a very different kind of painter was working in the Carmine church in Florence.

This was no gentle, refined monk, but just an ordinary man of the world—an awkward, good– natured person, who, as long as he had pictures to paint, cared for little else. Why, he would even forget to ask for payment when his work was done; and as to taking care of his clothes, or trying to keep himself tidy, that was a thing he never thought of!

What trouble his mother must have had with him when he was a boy! It was no use sending him on an errand, he would forget it before he had gone a hundred yards, and he was so careless and untidy that it was enough to make any one lose patience with him. But only let him have a pencil and a smooth surface on which to draw, and he was a different boy.

It is said that even now, in the little town of Castello San Giovanni, some eighteen miles from Florence, where Tommaso was born, there are still some wonderfully good figures to be seen, drawn by him when he was quite a little boy. Certainly there was no carelessness and nothing untidy about his work.

As the boy grew older all his longings would turn towards Florence, the beautiful city where there was everything to learn and to see, and so he was sent to become a pupil in the studio of Masolino, a great Florentine painter. But though his drawings improved, his careless habits continued the same.

`There goes Tommaso the painter,' the people would say, watching the big awkward figure passing through the streets on his way to work. `Truly he pays but little heed to his appearance. Look but at his untidy hair and the holes in his boots.'

`Ay, indeed!' another would answer; `and yet it is said if only people paid him all they owed he would have gold enough and to spare. But what cares he so long as he has his paints and brushes? ``Masaccio'' would be a fitter name for him than Tommaso.'

So the name Masaccio, or Ugly Tom, came to be that by which the big awkward painter was known. But no one thinks of the unkind meaning of the nickname now, for Masaccio is honoured as one of the great names in the history of Art.

This painter, careless of many things, cared with all his heart and soul for the work he had chosen to do. It seemed to him that painters had always failed to make their pictures like living things. The pictures they painted were flat, not round as a figure should be, and very often the feet did not look as if they were standing on the ground at all, but pointed downwards as if they were hanging in the air.

So he worked with light and shadow and careful drawing until the figures he drew looked rounded instead of flat, and their feet were planted firmly on the ground. His models were taken from the ordinary Florentine youths whom he saw daily in the studio, but he drew them as no one had drawn figures before. The buildings, too, he made to look like real houses leading away into the distance, and not just like a flat picture.

He painted many frescoes both in Florence and Rome, this Ugly Tom, but at the time the people did not pay him much honour, for they thought him just a great awkward fellow with his head always in the clouds. Perhaps if he had lived longer fame and wealth would have come to him, but he died when he was still a young man, and only a few realised how great he was.

But in after years, one by one, all the great artists would come to that little chapel of the Carmine there to learn their first lessons from those life–like figures. Especially they would stand before the fresco which shows St. Peter baptizing a crowd of people. And in that fresco they would study more than all the figure of a boy who has just come out of the water, shivering with cold, the most natural figure that had ever been painted up to that time.

All things must be learnt little by little, and each new thing we know is a step onwards. So this figure of the shivering boy marks a higher step of the golden ladder of Art than any that had been touched before. And this alone would have made the name of Masaccio worthy to be placed upon the list of world's great painters.

FRA FILIPPO LIPPI

It was winter time in Florence. The tramontana, that keen wind which blows from over the snow mountains, was sweeping down the narrow streets, searching out every nook and corner with its icy breath. Men flung their cloaks closer round them, and pulled their hats down over their eyes, so that only the tips of their noses were left uncovered for the wind to freeze. Women held their scaldinoes, little pots of hot charcoal, closer under their shawls, and even the dogs had a sad, half–frozen look. One and all longed for the warm winds of spring and the summer heat they loved. It was bad enough for those who had warm clothes and plenty of polenta, but for the poor life was very hard those cold wintry days.

In a doorway of a great house, in one of the narrow streets, a little boy of eight was crouching behind one of the stone pillars as he tried to keep out of the grip of the tramontana. His little coat was folded closely round him, but it was full of rents and holes so that the thin body inside was scarcely covered, and the child's blue lips trembled with the cold, and his black eyes filled with tears.

It was not often that Filippo turned such a sad little face to meet the world. Usually those black eyes sparkled with fun and mischief, and the mouth spread itself into a merry grin. But to−day, truly things were worse than he ever remembered them before, and he could remember fairly bad times, too, if he tried.

Other children had their fathers and mothers who gave them food and clothes, but he seemed to be quite different, and never had had any one to care for him. True, there was his aunt, old Mona Lapaccia, who said he had once had a father and mother like other boys, but she always added with a mournful shake of her head that she alone had endured all the trouble and worry of bringing him up since he was two years old. `Ah,' she would say, turning her eyes upwards, `the saints alone know what I have endured with a great hungry boy to feed and clothe.'

It seemed to Filippo that in that case the saints must also know how very little he had to eat, and how cold he was on these wintry days. But of course they would be too grand to care about a little boy.

In summer things were different. One could roll merrily about in the sunshine all day long, and at night sleep in some cool sheltering corner of the street. And then, too, there was always a better chance of picking up something to eat. Plenty of fig skins and melon parings were flung carelessly out into the street when fruit was plentiful, and people would often throw away the remains of a bunch of grapes. It was wonderful how quickly Filippo learned to know people's faces, and to guess who would finish to the last grape and who would throw the smaller ones away. Some would even smile as they caught his anxious, waiting eye fixed on the fruit, and would cry `Catch' as they threw a goodly bunch into those small brown hands that never let anything slip through their fingers.

Oh, yes, summer was all right, but there was always winter to face. To−day he was so very hungry, and the lupin skins which he had collected for his breakfast were all eaten long ago. He had hung about the little open shops, sniffing up the delicious smell of fried polenta, but no one had given him a morsel. All he had got was a stern `be off' when he ventured too close to the tempting food. If only this day had been a festa, he might have done well enough. For in the great processions when the priests and people carried their lighted candles round the church, he could always dart in and out with his little iron scraper, lift the melted wax of the marble floor and sell it over again to the candlemakers.

But there were no processions to–day, and there remained only one thing to be done. He must go home and see if Mona Lapaccia had anything to spare. Perhaps the saints took notice when he was hungry.

Down the street he ran, keeping close to the wall, just as the dogs do when it rains. For the great overhanging eaves of the houses act as a sheltering umbrella. Then out into the broad street that runs beside the river, where, even in winter, the sun shines warmly if it shines anywhere.

Filippo paused at the corner of the Ponte alla Carraja to watch the struggles of a poor mule which was trying to pull a huge cartload of wood up the steep incline of the bridge. It was so exciting that for a moment he forgot how cold and hungry he was, as he shouted and screamed directions with the rest of the crowd, darted in and out in his eagerness to help, and only got into every one's way.

That excitement over, Filippo felt in better spirits and ran quickly across the bridge. He soon threaded his way to a poor street that led towards one of the city gates, where everything looked dirtier and more cheerless than ever. He had not expected a welcome, and he certainly did not get one, as, after climbing the steep stairs, he cautiously pushed open the door and peeped in.

His aunt's thin face looked dark and angry. Poor soul, she had had no breakfast either, and there would be no food that day unless her work was finished. And here was this troublesome boy back again, when she thought she had got rid of him for the day

`Away!' she shouted crossly. `What dost thou mean by coming back so soon? Away, and seek thy living in the streets.'

`It is too cold,' said the boy, creeping into the bare room, `and I am hungry.'

`Hungry!' and poor Mona Lapaccia cast her eyes upwards, as if she would ask the saints if they too were not filled with surprise to hear this word. `And when art thou anything else? It is ever the same story with thee: eat, eat, eat. Now, the saints help me, I have borne this burden long enough. I will see if I cannot shift it on to other shoulders.'

She rose as she spoke, tied her yellow handkerchief over her head and smoothed out her apron. Then she caught Filippo by his shoulder and gave him a good shake, just to teach him how wrong it was to talk of being hungry, and pushing him in front of her they went downstairs together.

`Where art thou going?' gasped the boy as she dragged him swiftly along the street.

`Wait and thou shalt see,' she answered shortly; `and do thou mind thy manners, else will I mind them for thee.'

Filippo ran along a little quicker on hearing this advice. He had but a dim notion of what minding his manners might mean, but he guessed fairly well what would happen if his aunt minded them. Ah! here they were at the great square of the Carmine. He had often crept into the church to get warm and to see those wonderful pictures on the walls. Could they be going there now?

But it was towards the convent door that Mona Lapaccia bent her steps, and, when she had rung the bell, she gave Filippo's shoulder a final shake, and pulled his coat straight and smoothed his hair.

A fat, good−natured brother let them in, and led them through the many passages into a room where the prior sat finishing his midday meal.

Filippo's hungry eyes were immediately fixed on a piece of bread which lay upon the table, and the kindly prior smiled as he nodded his head towards it.

Not another invitation did Filippo need; like a bird he darted forward and snatched the piece of good white bread, and holding it in both hands he began to munch to his heart's content. How long it was since he had tasted anything like this! It was so delicious that for a few blissful moments he forgot where he was, forgot his aunt and the great man who was looking at him with such kind eyes.

But presently he heard his own name spoken and then he looked up and remembered. `And so, Filippo, thou wouldst become a monk?' the prior was saying. `Let me see—how old art thou?'

`Eight years old, your reverence,' said Mona Lapaccia before Filippo could answer. Which was just as well, as his mouth was still very full.

`And it is thy desire to leave the world, and enter our convent?' continued the prior. `Art thou willing to give up all, that thou mayest become a servant of God?'

The little dirty brown hands clutched the bread in dismay. Did the kind man mean that he was to give up his bread when he had scarcely eaten half of it?

`No, no; eat thy bread, child,' said the prior, with an understanding nod. `Thou art but a babe, but we will make a good monk of thee yet.'

Then, indeed, began happy days for Filippo. No more threadbare coats, but a warm little brown serge robe, tied round the waist with a rope whose ends grew daily shorter as the way round his waist grew longer. No more lupin skins and whiffs of fried polenta, but food enough and to spare; such food as he had not dreamt of before, and always as much as he could eat.

Filippo was as happy as the day was long. He had always been a merry little soul even when life had been hard and food scarce, and now he would not have changed his lot with the saints in Paradise.

But the good brothers began to think it was time Filippo should do something besides play and eat.

`Let us see what the child is fit for,' they said.

So Filippo was called in to sit on the bench with the boys and learn his A B C. That was dreadfully dull work. He could never remember the names of those queer signs. Their shapes he knew quite well, and he could draw them carefully in his copy– book, but their names were too much for him. And as to the Latin which the good monks tried to teach him, they might as well have tried to teach a monkey.

All the brightness faded from Filippo's face the moment a book was put before him, and he looked so dull and stupid that the brothers were in despair. Then for a little things seemed to improve. Filippo suddenly lost his stupid look as he bent over the pages, and his eyes were bright with interest.

`Aha!' said one brother nudging the other, `the boy has found his brains at last.'

But great indeed was their wrath and disappointment when they looked over his shoulder. Instead of learning his lessons, Filippo had been making all sorts of queer drawings round the margin of the page. The A's and B's had noses and eyes, and looked out with little grinning faces. The long music notes had legs and arms and were dancing about like little black imps. Everything was scribbled over with the naughty little figures.

This was really too much, and Filippo must be taken at once before the prior.

`What, in disgrace again?' asked the kindly old man. `What has the child done now?'

`We can teach him nothing,' said the brother, shaking a severe finger at Filippo, who hung his head. `He cannot even learn his A B C. And besides, he spoils his books, ay, and even the walls and benches, by drawing such things as these upon them.' And the indignant monk held out the book where all those naughty figures were dancing over the page.

The prior took the book and looked at it closely.

`What makes thee do these things?' he asked the boy, who stood first on one foot and then on the other, twisting his rope in his fingers.

At the sound of the kind voice, the boy looked up, and his face broke into a smile.

`Indeed, I cannot help it, Father,' he said. `It is the fault of these,' and he spread out his ten little brown fingers.

The prior laughed.

`Well,' he said, `we will not turn thee out, though they do say thou wilt never make a monk. Perhaps we may teach these ten little rascals to do good work, even if we cannot put learning into that round head of thine.'

So instead of books and Latin lessons, the good monks tried a different plan. Filippo was given as a pupil to good Brother Anselmo, whose work it was to draw the delicate pictures and letters for the convent prayer–books.

This was a different kind of lesson, indeed. Filippo's eyes shone with eagerness as he bent over his work and tried to copy the beautiful lines and curves which the master set for him.

There were other boys in the class as well, and Filippo looked at their work with great admiration. One boy especially, who was bigger than Filippo, and who had a kind merry face, made such beautiful copies that Filippo always tried to sit next him if possible. Very soon the boys became great friends.

Diamante, as the elder boy was called, was pleased to be admired so much by the little new pupil; but as time went on, his pride in his own work grew less as he saw with amazement how quickly Filippo's little brown fingers learned to draw straighter lines and more beautiful curves than any he could manage. Brother Anselmo, too, would watch the boy at work, and his saintly old face beamed with pleasure as he looked.

`He will pass us all, and leave us far behind, this child who is too stupid to learn his A B C,' he would say, and his face shone with unselfish joy.

Then when the boys grew older, they were allowed to go into the church and watch those wonderful frescoes, which grew under the hand of the great awkward painter, `Ugly Tom,' as he was called.

Together Filippo and Diamante stood and watched with awe, learning lessons there which the good father had not been able to teach. Then they would begin to put into practice what they had learned, and try to copy in their own pictures the work of the great master.

`Thou hast the knack of it, Filippo,' Diamante would say as he looked with envy at the figures Filippo drew so easily.

`Thy pictures are also good,' Filippo would answer quickly, `and thou thyself art better than any one else in the convent.'

There was no complaint now of Filippo's dullness. He soon learned all that the painter—monks could teach him, and as years passed on the prior would rub his hands in delight to think that here was an artist, one of themselves, who would soon be able to paint the walls of the church and convent, and make them as famous as the convent of San Marco had been made famous by its angelical painter.

Then one day he called Filippo to him.

`My son,' he said, `you have learned well, and it is time now to turn your work to some account. Go into the cloister where the walls have been but newly whitewashed, and let us see what kind of pictures thou canst paint.'

With burning cheeks and shining eyes, Filippo began his work. Day after day he stood on the scaffolding, with his brown robe pinned back and his bare arm moving swiftly as he drew figure after figure on the smooth white wall.

He did not pause to think what he would draw, the figures seemed to grow like magic under his touch. There were the monks in their brown and white robes, fat and laughing, or lean and anxious– minded. There were the people who came to say their prayers in church, little children clinging to their mothers' skirts, beggars and rich folks, even the stray dog that sometimes wandered in. Yes, and the pretty girls who laughed and talked in whispers. He drew them all, just as he had often seen them. Then, when the last piece of wall was covered, he stopped his work.

The news soon spread through all the convent that Brother Filippo had finished his picture, and all the monks came hurrying to see. The scaffolding was taken down, and then they all stood round, gazing with round eyes and open mouths. They had never seen anything like it before, and at first there was silence except for one long drawn `ah–h.'

Then one by one they began to laugh and talk, and point with eager, excited fingers. `Look,' cried one, `there is Brother Giovanni; I would know his smile among a hundred.'

`There is that beggar who comes each day to ask for soup,' cried another.

`And there is his dog,' shouted a third.

`Look at the maid who kneels in front,' said Fra Diamante in a hushed voice, `is she not as fair as any saint?'

Then suddenly there was silence, and the brothers looked ashamed of the noise they had been making, as the prior himself looked down on them from the steps above.

`What is all this?' he asked. And his voice sounded grave and displeased as he looked from the wall to the crowd of eager monks. Then he turned to Filippo. `Are these the pictures I ordered thee to paint?' he asked. `Is this the kind of painting to do honour to God and to our Church? Will these mere human figures help men to remember the saints, teach them to look up to heaven, or help them with their prayers? Quick, rub them out, and paint your pictures for heaven and not for earth.'

Filippo hung his head, the crowd of admiring monks swiftly disappeared, and he was left to begin his work all over again.

It was so difficult for Filippo to keep his thoughts fixed on heaven, and not to think of earth. He did so love the merry world, and his fingers, those same ten brown rascals which had got him into trouble when he was a child, always longed to draw just the faces that he saw every day. The pretty face of the little maid kneeling at her prayers was so real and so delightful, and the Madonna and angels seemed so solemn and far off.

Still no one would have pictures which did not tell of saints and angels, so he must paint the best he could. After all, it was easy to put on wings and golden haloes until the earthly things took on a heavenly look.

But the convent life grew daily more and more wearisome now to Filippo. The world, which he had been so willing to give up for a piece of good white bread when he was eight years old, now seemed full of all the things he loved best.

25

The more he thought of it, the more he longed to see other places outside the convent walls, and other faces besides the monks and the people who came to church.

And so one dark night, when all the brothers were asleep and the bells had just rung the midnight hour, Fra Filippo stole out of his cell, unlocked the convent door, and ran swiftly out into the quiet street.

How good it felt to be free! The very street itself seemed like an old friend, welcoming him with open arms. On and on he ran until he came to the city gates of San Frediano, there to wait until he could slip through unnoticed when the gates were opened at the dawn of day. Then on again until Florence and the convent were left behind and the whole world lay before him.

There was no difficulty about living, for the people gave him food and money, and good−natured countrymen would stop their carts and offer him a lift along the straight white dusty roads. So by and by he reached Ancona and saw for the first time the sea.

Filippo gazed and gazed, forgetting everything else as he drank in the beauty of that great stretch of quivering blue, while in his ears sounded words which he had almost forgotten—words which had fallen on heedless ears at matins or vespers—and which never had held any meaning for him before: `And before the throne was a sea of glass, like unto crystal.'

He stood still for a few minutes and then the heavenly vision faded, and like any other boy he forgot all about beauty and colour, and only longed to be out in a boat enjoying the strange new delight.

Very lucky he thought himself when he reached the shore to find a boat just putting of, and to hear himself invited to jump in by the boys who were going for a sail.

Away they went, further and further from the shore, laughing and talking. The boys were so busy telling wonderful sea−tales to the young stranger that they did not notice how far they had gone. Then suddenly they looked ahead and sat speechless with fear.

A great Moorish galley was bearing down upon them, its rows of oars flashed in the sunlight, and its great painted sails towered above their heads. It was no use trying to escape. Those strong rowers easily overtook them, and in a few minutes Filippo and his companions were hoisted up on board the galley.

It was all so sudden that it seemed like a dream. But the chains were very real that were fastened round their wrists and ankles, and the dark cruel faces of the Moors as they looked on smiling at their misery were certainly no dream.

Then followed long days of misery when the new slaves toiled at the oars under the blazing sun, and nights of cold and weariness. Many a time did Filippo long for the quiet convent, the kindly brothers, and the long peaceful days. Many a time did he long to hear the bells calling him to prayer, which had once only filled him with restless impatience.

But at last the galley reached the coast of Barbary, and the slaves were unchained from the oars and taken ashore. In all his misery Filippo's keen eyes still watched with interest the people around him, and he was never tired of studying the swarthy faces and curious garments of the Moorish pirates.

Then one day when he happened to be near a smooth white wall, he took a charred stick from a fire which was built close by, and began to draw the figure of his master.

What a delight it was to draw those rapid strokes and feel the likeness grow beneath his fingers! He was so much interested that he did not notice the crowd that gathered gradually round him, but he worked steadily on until the figure was finished.

Just as the band of monks had stood silent round his first picture in the cloister of the Carmine, so these dark Moors stood still in wonder and amazement gazing upon the bold black figure sketched upon the smooth white wall.

No one had ever seen such a thing in that land before, and it seemed to them that this man must be a dealer in magic. They whispered together, and one went off hurriedly to fetch the captain.

The master, when he came, was as astonished as the men. He could scarcely believe his eyes when he saw a second self drawn upon the wall, more like than his own shadow. This indeed must be no common man; and he ordered that Filippo's chains should be immediately struck off, and that he should be treated with respect and honour.

Nothing now was too good for this man of magic, and before long Filippo was put on board a ship and carried safely back to Italy. They put him ashore at Naples, and for some little time Filippo stayed there painting pictures for the king; but his heart was in his own beloved town, and very soon he returned to Florence.

Perhaps he did not deserve a welcome, but every one was only too delighted to think that the runaway had really returned. Even the prior, though he shook his head, was glad to welcome back the brother whose painting had already brought fame and honour to the convent.

But in spite of all the troubles Filippo had gone through, he still dearly loved the merry world and all its pleasures. For a long time he would paint his saints and angels with all due diligence, and then he would dash down brushes and pencils, leave his paints scattered around, and of he would go for a holiday. Then the work would come to a stand– still, and people must just wait until Filippo should feel inclined to begin again.

The great Cosimo de Medici, who was always the friend of painters, desired above all things that Fra Filippo should paint a picture for him. And what is more, having heard so many tales about the idle ways of this same brother, he was determined that the picture should be painted without any interruptions.

`Fra Filippo shall take no holidays while at work for me,' he said, as he talked the matter over with the prior.

`That may not be so easy as thou thinkest,' said the prior, for he knew Filippo better than did this great Cosimo.

But Cosimo did not see any difficulty in the matter whatever. High in his palace he prepared a room for the painter, and placed there everything he could need. No comfort was lacking, and when Filippo came he was treated as an honoured guest, except for one thing. Whenever the heavy door of his room swung to, there was a grating sound heard, and the key in the lock was turned from outside. So Filippo was really a captive in his handsome prison.

That was all very well for a few days. Filippo laughed as he painted away, and laid on the tender blue of the Virgin's robe, and painted into her eyes the solemn look which he had so often seen on the face of some poor peasant woman as she knelt at prayer. But after a while he grew restless and weary of his work.

`Plague take this great man and his fine manners,' he cried. `Does he think he can catch a lark and train it to sing in a cage at his bidding? I am weary of saints and angels. I must out to breathe the fresh sweet air of heaven.'

But the key was always turned in the lock and the door was strong. There was the window, but it was high above the street, and the grey walls, built of huge square stones, might well have been intended to enclose a prison rather than a palace.

It was a dark night, and the air felt hot as Filippo leaned out of the window. Scarce a breath stirred the still air, and every sound could be heard distinctly. Far below in the street he could hear the tread of the people's feet, and catch the words of a merry song as a company of boys and girls danced merrily along.

`Flower of the rose, If I've been happy, what matter who knows,'

they sang.

It was all too tempting; out he must get. Filippo looked round his room, and his eye rested on the bed. With a shout of triumphant delight he ran towards it. First he seized the quilt and tore it into strips, then the blankets, then the sheets.

`Whoever saw a grander rope?' he chuckled to himself as he knotted the ends together.

Quick as thought he tied it to the iron bar that ran across his window, and, squeezing out, he began to climb down, hand over hand, dangling and swinging to and fro. The rope was stout and good, and now he could steady himself by catching his toes in the great iron rings fastened into the wall, until at last he dropped breathless into the street below.

Next day, when Cosimo came to see how the painting went on, he saw indeed the pictures and the brushes, but no painter was there. Quickly he stepped to the open window, and there he saw the dangling rope of sheets, and guessed at once how the bird had flown.

Through the streets they searched for the missing painter, and before long he was found and brought back. Filippo tried to look penitent, but his eyes were dancing with merriment, and Cosimo must needs laugh too.

`After all,' said Filippo, `my talent is not like a beast of burden, to be driven and beaten into doing its work. It is rather like one of those heavenly visitors whom we willingly entertain when they deign to visit us, but whom we can never force either to come or go at will.'

`Thou art right, friend painter,' answered the great man. `And when I think how thou and thy talent might have taken wings together, had not the rope held good, I vow I will never seek to keep thee in against thy will again.'

`Then will I work all the more willingly,' answered Filippo.

So with doors open, and freedom to come and go, Filippo no longer wished to escape, but worked with all his heart. The beautiful Madonna and angel were soon finished, and besides he painted a wonderful picture of seven saints with St. John sitting in their midst.

From far and near came requests that Fra Filippo Lippi should paint pictures for different churches and convents. He would much rather have painted the scenes and the people he saw every day, but he remembered the prior's lecture, and still painted only the stories of saints and holy people—the gentle Madonna with her scarlet book of prayers, the dove fluttering near, and the angel messenger with shining wings bearing the lily branch. True, the saints would sometimes look out of his pictures with the faces of some of his friends, but no one seemed to notice that. On the whole his was a happy life, and he was always ready to paint for any one that should ask him.

Many people now were proud to know the famous young painter, but his old companion Fra Diamante was still the friend he loved best. Whenever it was possible they still would work together; so, great was their delight when one day an order came from Prato that they should both go there to paint the walls of San Stefano.

`Good−bye to old Florence for a while,' cried Filippo as they set out merrily together. He looked back as he spoke at the spires and sunbaked roofs, the white marble facade of San Miniato, and the dark cypresses standing clear against the pure warm sky of early spring.

`I am weary of your great men and all your pomp and splendour. Something tells me we shall have a golden time among the good folk of Prato.'

Perhaps it was the springtime that made Filippo so joyous that morning as he rode along the dusty white road.

Spring had come with a glad rush, as she ever comes in Italy, scattering on every side her flowers and favours. From under the dead brown leaves of autumn, violets pushed their heads and perfumed all the air. Under the grey olives the sprouting corn spread its tender green, and the scarlet and purple of the anemones waved spring's banner far and near. It was good to be alive on such a day.

Arrived at Prato, the two painters, with a favourite pupil called Botticelli, worked together diligently, and covered wall after wall with their frescoes. It seemed as if they would never be done, for each church and convent had work awaiting them.

`Truly,' said Filippo one day when he was putting the last touches to a portrait of Fra Diamante, whom he had painted into his picture of the death of St. Stephen, `I will undertake no more work for a while. It is full time we had a holiday together.'

But even as he spoke a message was brought to him from the good abbess of the convent of Santa Margherita, begging him to come and paint an altarpiece for the sisters' chapel.

`Ah, well, what must be, must be,' he said to Fra Diamante, who stood smiling by. `I will do what I can to please these holy women, but after that—no more.'

The staid and sober abbess met him at the convent door, and silently led him through the sunny garden, bright with flowers, where the lizards darted to right and left as they walked past the fountain and entered the dim, cool chapel. In a low, sweet voice she told him what they would have him paint, and showed him the space above the high altar where the picture was to be placed.

`Our great desire is that thou shouldst paint for us the Holy Virgin with the Blessed Child on the night of the Nativity,' she said.

The painter seemed to listen, but his attention wandered, and all the time he wished himself back in the sunny garden, where he had seen a fair young face looking through the pink sprays of almond blossoms, while the music of the vesper hymn sounded sweet and clear in his ears.

`I will begin to–morrow,' he said with a start when the low voice of the abbess stopped. `I will paint the Madonna and Babe as thou desirest.'

So next day the work began. And each time the abbess noiselessly entered the room where the painter was at work and watched the picture grow beneath his hand, she felt more and more sure that she had done right in asking this painter to decorate their beloved chapel.

True, it was said by many that the young artist was but a worldly minded man, not like the blessed Fra Angelico, the heavenly painter of San Marco; but his work was truly wonderful, and his handsome face looked good, even if a somewhat merry smile was ever wont to lurk about his mouth and in his eyes.

Then came a morning when the abbess found Filippo standing idle, with a discontented look upon his face. He was gazing at the unfinished picture, and for a while he did not see that any one had entered the room.

`Is aught amiss?' asked the gentle voice at his side, and Filippo turned and saw the abbess.

`Something indeed seems amiss with my five fingers,' said Filippo, with his quick bright smile. `Time after time have I tried to paint the face of the Madonna, and each time I must needs paint it out again.'

Then a happy thought came into his mind.

`I have seen a face sometimes as I passed through the convent garden which is exactly what I want,' he cried. `If thou wouldst but let the maiden sit where I can see her for a few hours each day, I can promise thee that the Madonna will be finished as thou wouldst wish.'

The abbess stood in deep thought for a few minutes, for she was puzzled to know what she should do.

`It is the child Lucrezia,' she thought to herself. `She who was sent here by her father, the noble Buti of Florence. She is but a novice still, and there can be no harm in allowing her to lend her fair face as a model for Our Lady.'

So she told Filippo it should be as he wished.

It was dull in the convent, and Lucrezia was only too pleased to spend some hours every morning, idly sitting in the great chair, while the young painter talked to her and told her stories while he painted. She counted the hours until it was time to go back, and grew happier each day as the Madonna's face grew more and more beautiful.

Surely there was no one so good or so handsome as this wonderful artist. Lucrezia could not bear to think how dull her life would be when he was gone. Then one day, when it happened that the abbess was called away and they were alone, Filippo told Lucrezia that he loved her and could not live without her; and although she was frightened at first, she soon grew happy, and told him that she was ready to go with him wherever he wished. But what would the good nuns think of it? Would they ever let her go? No; they must think of some other plan.

To—morrow was the great festa of Prato, when all the nuns walked in procession to see the holy centola, or girdle, which the Madonna had given to St. Thomas. Lucrezia must take care to walk on the outside of the procession, and to watch for a touch upon the arm as she passed.

The festa day dawned bright and clear, and all Prato was early astir. Procession after procession wound its way to the church where the relic was to be shown, and the crowd grew denser every moment. Presently came the nuns of Santa Margherita. A figure in the crowd pressed nearer. Lucrezia felt a touch upon her arm, and a strong hand clasped hers. The crowd swayed to and fro, and in an instant the two figures disappeared. No one noticed that the young novice was gone, and before the nuns thought of looking for their charge Lucrezia was on her way to Florence, her horse led by the painter whom she loved, while his good friend Fra Diamante rode beside her.

Then the storm burst. Lucrezia's father was furious, the good nuns were dismayed, and every one shook their heads over this last adventure of the Florentine painter.

But luckily for Filippo, the great Cosimo still stood his friend and helped him through it all. He it was who begged the Pope to allow Fra Filippo to marry Lucrezia (for monks, of course, were never allowed to marry), and the Pope, too, was kind and granted the request, so that all went well.

Now indeed was Lucrezia as happy as the day was long, and when the spring returned once more to Florence, a baby Filippo came with the violets and lilies.

`How wilt thou know us apart if thou callest him Filippo?' asked the proud father.

`Ah, he is such a little one, dear heart,' Lucrezia answered gaily. `We will call him Filippino, and then there can be no mistake.'

There was no more need now to seek for pleasures out of doors. Filippo painted his pictures and lived his happy home life without seeking any more adventures. His Madonnas grew ever more beautiful, for they were all touched with the beauty that shone from Lucrezia's fair face, and the Infant Christ had ever the smile and the curly golden hair of the baby Filippino.

And by and by a little daughter came to gladden their hearts, and then indeed their cup of joy was full.

`What name shall we give the little maid?' said Filippo.

`Methought thou wouldst have it Lucrezia,' answered the mother.

`There is but one Lucrezia in all the world for me,' he said. `None other but thee shall bear that name.'

As they talked a knock sounded at the door, and presently the favourite pupil, Sandro, looked in. There was a shout of joy from little Filippino, and the young man lifted the child in his arms and smiled with the look of one who loves children.

`Come, Sandro, and see the little new flower,' said Filippo. `Is she not as fair as the roses which thou dost so love to paint?'

Then, as the young man looked with interest at the tiny face, Filippo clapped him on the shoulder.

`I have it!' he cried. `She shall be called after thee, Alessandra. Some day she will be proud to think that she bears thy name.'

For already Filippo knew that this pupil of his would ere long wake the world to new wonder.

The only clouds that hid the sunshine of Lucrezia's life was when Filippo was obliged to leave her for a while and paint his pictures in other towns. She always grew sad when his work in Florence drew to a close, for she never knew where his next work might lie.

`Well,' said Filippo one night as he returned home and caught up little Filippino in his arms, `the picture for the nuns of San Ambrogio is finished at last! Truly they have saints and angels enough this time—rows upon rows of sweet faces and white lilies. And the sweetest face of all is thine, Saint Lucy, kneeling in front with thy hand beneath the chin of this young cherub.'

`Is it indeed finished so soon?' asked Lucrezia, a wistful note creeping into her voice.

`Ay, and to-morrow I must away to Spoleto to begin my work at the Chapel of Our Lady. But look not so sad, dear heart; before three months are past, by the time the grapes are gathered, I will return.'

But it was sad work parting, though it might only be for three months, and even her little son could not make his mother smile, though he drew wonderful pictures for her of birds and beasts, and told her he meant to be a great painter like his father when he grew up.

Next day Filippo started, and with him went his good friend Fra Diamante.

`Fare thee well, Filippo. Take good care of him, friend Diamante,' cried Lucrezia; and she stood watching until their figures disappeared at the end of the long white road, and then went inside to wait patiently for their return.

The summer days passed slowly by. The cheeks of the peaches grew soft and pink under the kiss of the sun, the figs showed ripe and purple beneath the green leaves, and the grapes hung in great transparent clusters of purple and gold from the vines that swung between the poplar–trees. Then came the merry days of vintage, and the juice was pressed out of the ripe grapes.

`Now he will come back,' said Lucrezia, `for he said ``by the time the grapes are gathered I will return." '

The days went slowly by, and every evening she stood in the loggia and gazed across the hills. Then she would point out the long white road to little Filippino.

`Thy father will come along that road ere long,' she said, and joy sang in her voice.

Then one evening as she watched as usual her heart beat quickly. Surely that figure riding so slowly along was Fra Diamante? But where was Filippo, and why did his friend ride so slowly?

When he came near and entered the house she looked into his face, and all the joy faded from her eyes.

`You need not tell me,' she cried; `I know that Filippo is dead.'

It was but too true. The faithful friend had brought the sad news himself. No one could tell how Filippo had died. A few short hours of pain and then all was over. Some talked of poison. But who could tell?

There had just been time to send his farewell to Lucrezia, and to pray his friend to take charge of little Filippino.

So, as she listened, joy died out of Lucrezia's life. Spring might come again, and summer sunshine make others glad, but for her it would be ever cold, bleak winter. For never more should her heart grow warm in the sunshine of Filippo's smile—that sunshine which had made every one love him, in spite of his faults, ever since he ran about the streets, a little ragged boy, in the old city of Florence.

SANDRO BOTTICELLI

We must now go back to the days when Fra Filippo Lippi painted his pictures and so brought fame to the Carmine Convent.

There was at that time in Florence a good citizen called Mariano Filipepi, an honest, well-to-do man, who had several sons. These sons were all taught carefully and well trained to do each the work he chose. But the fourth son, Alessandro, or Sandro as he was called, was a great trial to his father. He would settle to no trade or calling. Restless and uncertain, he turned from one thing to another. At one time he would work with all his might, and then again become as idle and fitful as the summer breeze. He could learn well and quickly when he chose, but then there were so few things that he did choose to learn. Music he loved, and he knew every song of the birds, and anything connected with flowers was a special joy to him. No one knew better than he how the different kinds of roses grew, and how the lilies hung upon their stalks.

`And what, I should like to know, is going to be the use of all this,' the good father would say impatiently, `as long as thou takest no pains to read and write and do thy sums? What am I to do with such a boy, I wonder?'

Then in despair the poor man decided to send Sandro to a neighbour's workshop, to see if perhaps his hands would work better than his head.

The name of this neighbour was Botticelli, and he was a goldsmith, and a very excellent master of his art. He agreed to receive Sandro as his pupil, so it happened that the boy was called by his master's name, and was known ever after as Sandro Botticelli.

Sandro worked for some time with his master, and quickly learned to draw designs for the goldsmith's work.

In those days painters and goldsmiths worked a great deal together, and Sandro often saw designs for pictures and listened to the talk of the artists who came to his master's shop. Gradually, as he looked and listened, his mind was made up. He would become a painter.

All his restless longings and day dreams turned to this. All the music that floated in the air as he listened to the birds' song, the gentle dancing motion of the wind among the trees, all the colours of the flowers, and the graceful twinings of the rose–stems—all these he would catch and weave into his pictures. Yes, he would learn to painst music and motion, and then he would be happy.

`So now thou wilt become a painter,' said his father, with a hopeless sigh.

Truly this boy was more trouble than all the rest put together. Here he had just settled down to learn how to become a good goldsmith, and now he wished to try his hand at something else. Well, it was no use saying `no.' The boy could never be made to do anything but what he wished. There was the Carmelite monk Fra Filippo Lippi, of whom all, men were talking. It was said he was the greatest painter in Florence. The boy should have the best teaching it was possible to give him, and perhaps this time he would stick to his work.

So Sandro was sent as a pupil to Fra Filippo, and he soon became a great favourite with the happy, sunny–tempered master. The quick eye of the painter soon saw that this was no ordinary pupil. There was something about Sandro's drawing that was different to anything that Filippo had ever seen before. His figures seemed to move, and one almost heard the wind rustling in their flowing drapery. Instead of walking, they seemed to be dancing lightly along with a swaying motion as if to the rhythm of music. The very rose–leaves the boy loved to paint, seemed to flutter down to the sound of a fairy song. Filippo was proud of his pupil.

`The world will one day hear more of my Sandro Botticelli,' he said; and, young though the boy was, he often took him to different places to help him in his work.

So it happened that, in that wonderful spring of Filippo's life, Sandro too was at Prato, and worked there with Fra Diamante. And in after years when the master's little daughter was born, she was named Alessandra, after the favourite pupil, to whom was also left the training of little Filippino.

Now, indeed, Sandros good old father had no further cause to complain. The boy had found the work he was most fitted for, and his name soon became famous in Florence.

It was the reign of gaiety and pleasure in the city of Florence at that time. Lorenzo the Magnificent, the son of Cosimo de Medici, was ruler now, and his court was the centre of all that was most splendid and beautiful. Rich dresses, dainty food, music, gay revels, everything that could give pleasure, whether good or bad, was there.

Lorenzo, like his father, was always glad to discover a new painter, and Botticelli soon became a great favourite at court.

But pictures of saints and angels were somewhat out of fashion at that time, for people did not care to be reminded of anything but earthly pleasures. So Botticelli chose his subjects to please the court, and for a while ceased to paint his sad–eyed Madonnas.

What mattered to him what his subject was? Let him but paint his dancing figures, tripping along in their light flowing garments, keeping time to the music of his thoughts, and the subject might be one of the old Greek tales or any other story that served his purpose.

All the gay court dresses, the rich quaint robes of the fair ladies, helped to train the young painter's fancy for flowing draperies and wonderful veils of filmy transparent gauze.

There was one fair lady especially whom Sandro loved to paint—the beautiful Simonetta, as she is still called.

First he painted her as Venus, who was born of the sea foam. In his picture she floats to the shore standing in a shell, her golden hair wrapped round her. The winds behind blow her onward and scatter pink and red roses through the air. On the shore stands Spring, who holds out a mantle, flowers nestling in its folds, ready to enwrap the goddess when the winds shall have wafted her to land.

Then again we see her in his wonderful picture of `Spring,' and in another called `Mars and Venus.' She was too great a lady to stoop to the humble painter, and he perhaps only looked up to her as a star shining in heaven, far out of the reach of his love. But he never ceased to worship her from afar. He never married or cared for any other fair face, just as the great poet Dante, whom Botticelli admired so much, dreamed only of his one love, Beatrice.

But Sandro did not go sadly through life sighing for what could never be his. He was kindly and good–natured, full of jokes, and ready to make merry with his pupils in the workshop.

It once happened that one of these pupils, Biagio by name, had made a copy of one of Sandro's pictures, a beautiful Madonna surrounded by eight angels. This he was very anxious to sell, and the master kindly promised to help him, and in the end arranged the matter with a citizen of Florence, who offered to buy it for six gold pieces.

`Well, Biagio,' said Sandro, when his pupil came into the studio next morning, `I have sold thy picture. Let us now hang it up in a good light that the man who wishes to buy it may see it at its best. Then will he pay thee the money.'

Biagio was overjoyed.

`Oh, master,' he cried, `how well thou hast done.'

Then with hands which trembled with excitement the pupil arranged the picture in the best light, and went to fetch the purchaser.

Now meanwhile Botticelli and his other pupils had made eight caps of scarlet pasteboard such as the citizens of Florence then wore, and these they fastened with wax on to the heads of the eight angels in the picture.

Presently Biagio came back panting with joyful excitement, and brought with him the citizen, who knew already of the joke. The poor boy looked at his picture and then rubbed his eyes. What had happened? Where were his angels? The picture must be bewitched, for instead of his angels he saw only eight citizens in scarlet caps.

He looked wildly around, and then at the face of the man who had promised to buy the picture. Of course he would refuse to take such a thing.

But, to his surprise, the citizen looked well pleased, and even praised the work.

`It is well worth the money,' he said; `and if thou wilt return with me to my house, I will pay thee the six gold pieces.'

Biagio scarcely knew what to do. He was so puzzled and bewildered he felt as if this must be a bad dream.

As soon as he could, he rushed back to the studio to look again at that picture, and then he found that the red–capped citizens had disappeared, and his eight angels were there instead. This of course was not surprising, as Sandro and his pupils had quickly removed the wax and taken off the scarlet caps.

`Master, master,' cried the astonished pupil, `tell me if I am dreaming, or if I have lost my wits? When I came in just now, these angels were Florentine citizens with red caps on their heads, and now they are angels once more. What may this mean?'

`I think, Biagio, that this money must have turned thy brain round,' said Botticelli gravely. `If the angels had looked as thou sayest, dost thou think the citizen would have bought the picture?'

`That is true,' said Biagio, shaking his head solemnly; `and yet I swear I never saw anything more clearly.'

And the poor boy, for many a long day, was afraid to trust his own eyes, since they had so basely deceived him.

But the next thing that happened at the studio did not seem like a joke to the master, for a weaver of cloth came to live close by, and his looms made such a noise and such a shaking that Sandro was deafened, and the house shook so greatly that it was impossible to paint.

But though Botticelli went to the weaver and explained all this most courteously, the man answered roughly, `Can I not do what I like with my own house?' So Sandro was angry, and went away and immediately ordered a great square of stone to be brought, so big that it filled a waggon. This he had placed on the top of his wall nearest to the weaver's house, in such a way that the least shake would bring it crashing down into the enemy's workshop.

When the weaver saw this he was terrified, and came round at once to the studio.

`Take down that great stone at once,' he shouted. `Do you not see that it would crush me and my workshop if it fell?'

`Not at all,' said Botticelli. `Why should I take it down? Can I not do as I like with my own house?'

And this taught the weaver a lesson, so that he made less noise and shaking, and Sandro had the best of the joke after all.

There were no idle days of dreaming now for Sandro. As soon as one picture was finished another was wanted. Money flowed in, and his purse was always full of gold, though he emptied it almost as fast as it was filled. His work for the Pope at Rome alone was so well paid that the money should have lasted him for many a long day, but in his usual careless way he spent it all before he returned to Florence.

Perhaps it was the gay life at Lorenzo's splendid court that had taught him to spend money so carelessly, and to have no thought but to eat, drink, and be merry. But very soon a change began to steal over his life.

There was one man in Florence who looked with sad condemning eyes on all the pleasure-loving crowd that thronged the court of Lorenzo the Magnificent. In the peaceful convent of San Marco, whose walls the angel-painter had covered with pictures `like windows into heaven,' the stern monk Savonarola was grieving over the sin and vanity that went on around him. He loved Florence with all his heart, and he could not bear the thought that she was forgetting, in the whirl of pleasure, all that was good and pure and worth the winning.

Then, like a battle-cry, his voice sounded through the city, and roused the people from their foolish dreams of ease and pleasure. Every one flocked to the great cathedral to hear Savonarola preach, and Sandro Botticelli left for a while his studio and his painting and became a follower of the great preacher. Never again did he paint those pictures of earthly subjects which had so delighted Lorenzo. When he once more returned to his work, it was to paint his sad-eyed Madonnas; and the music which still floated through his visions was now like the song of angels.

The boys of Florence especially had grown wild and rough during the reign of pleasure, and they were the terror of the city during carnival time. They would carry long poles, or `stili,' and bar the streets across, demanding money before they would let the people pass. This money they spent on drinking and feasting, and at night they set up great trees in the squares or wider streets and lighted huge bonfires around them. Then would begin a terrible fight with stones, and many of the boys were hurt, and some even killed.

No one had been able to put a stop to this until Savonarola made up his mind that it should cease. Then, as if by magic, all was changed.

Instead of the rough game of `stili,' there were altars put up at the corners of the streets, and the boys begged money of the passers–by, not for their feasts, but for the poor.

`You shall not miss your bonfire,' said Savonarola; `but instead of a tree you shall burn up vain and useless things, and so purify the city.'

So the children went round and collected all the `vanities,' as they were called—wigs and masks and carnival dresses, foolish songs, bad books, and evil pictures; all were heaped high and then lighted to make one great bonfire.

Some people think that perhaps Sandro threw into the Bonfire of Vanities some of his own beautiful pictures, but that we cannot tell.

Then came the sad time when the people, who at one time would have made Savonarola their king, turned against him, in the same fickle way that crowds will ever turn. And then the great preacher, who had spent his life trying to help and teach them, and to do them good, was burned in the great square of that city which he had loved so dearly.

After this it was long before Botticelli cared to paint again. He was old and weary now, poor and sad, sick of that world which had treated with such cruelty the master whom he loved.

One last picture he painted to show the triumph of good over evil. Not with the sword or the might of great power is the triumph won, says Sandro to us by this picture, but by the little hand of the Christ Child, conquering by love and drawing all men to Him. This Adoration of the Magi is in our own National Gallery in London, and is the only painting which Botticelli ever signed.

`I, Alessandro, painted this picture during the troubles of Italy ... when the devil was let loose for the space of three and a half years. Afterwards shall he be chained, and we shall see him trodden down as in this picture.'

It is evident that Botticelli meant by this those sad years of struggle against evil which ended in the martyrdom of the great preacher, and he has placed Savonarola among the crowd of worshippers drawn to His feet by the Infant Christ.

It is sad to think of those last days when Sandro was too old and too weary to paint. He who had loved to make his figures move with dancing feet, was now obliged to walk with crutches. The roses and lilies of spring were faded now, and instead of the music of his youth he heard only the sound of harsh, ungrateful voices, in the flowerless days of poverty and old age.

There is always something sad too about his pictures, but through the sadness, if we listen, we may hear the angel–song, and understand it better if we have in our minds the prayer which Botticelli left for us.

`Oh, King of Wings and Lord of Lords, who alone rulest always in eternity, and who correctest all our wanderings, giver of melody to the choir of angels, listen Thou a little to our bitter grief, and come and rule us, oh Thou highest King, with Thy love which is so sweet.'

DOMENICO GHIRLANDAIO

Ghirlandaio! what a difficult name that sounds to our English ears. But it has a very simple meaning, and when you understand it the difficulty will vanish.

It all happened in this way. Domenico's father was a goldsmith, one of the cleverest goldsmiths in Florence, and he was specially famous for making garlands or wreaths of gold and silver. It was the fashion then for the young maidens of Florence to wear these garlands, or `ghirlande' as they were called, on their heads, and because this goldsmith made them better than any one else they gave him the name of Ghirlandaio, which means `maker of garlands,' and that became the family name.

When the time came for the boy Domenico to learn a trade, he was sent, of course, to his father's workshop. He learned so quickly, and worked with such strong, clever fingers, that his father was delighted.

`The boy will make the finest goldsmith of his day,' he said proudly, as he watched him twisting the delicate golden wire and working out his designs in beaten silver.

So he was set to make the garlands, and for a while be was contented and happy. It was such exquisite work to twine into shape the graceful golden leaves, with here and there a silver lily or a jewelled rose, and to dream of the fair head on which the garland would rest.

But the making of garlands did not satisfy Domenico for long, and like Botticelli he soon began to dream of becoming a painter.

You must remember that in those days goldsmiths and painters had much in common, and often worked together. The goldsmith made his picture with gold and silver and jewels, while the painter drew his with colours, but they were both artists.

So as the young Ghirlandaio watched these men draw their great designs and listened to their talk, he began to feel that the goldsmith's work was cramped and narrow, and he longed for a larger, grander work. Day by day the garlands were more and more neglected, and every spare moment was spent drawing the faces of those who came to the shop, or even those of the passers–by.

But although, ere long, Ghirlandaio left his father's shop and learned to make pictures with colours, instead of with gold, silver, and jewels, still the training he had received in his goldsmith's work showed to the end in all his pictures. He painted the smallest things with extreme care, and was never tired of spreading them over with delicate ornaments and decorations. It is a great deal the outward show with Ghirlandaio, and not so much the inward soul, that we find in his pictures, though he had a wonderful gift of painting portraits.

These portraits painted by the young Ghirlandaio seemed very wonderful to the admiring Florentines. From all his pictures looked out faces which they knew and recognised immediately. There, in a group of saints, or in a crowd of figures around the Infant Christ, they saw the well-known faces of Florentine nobles, the great ladies from the palaces, ay, and even the men of the market-place, and the poor peasant women who sold eggs and vegetables in the streets. Once he painted an old bishop with a pair of spectacles resting on his nose. It was the first time that spectacles had ever been put into a picture.

Then off he must go to Rome, like every one else, to add his share to the famous frescoes of the Vatican. But it was in Florence that most of his work was done.

In the church of Santa Maria Novella there was a great chapel which belonged to the Ricci family. It had once been covered by beautiful frescoes, but now it was spoilt by damp and the rain that came through the leaking roof. The noble family, to whom the chapel belonged, were poor and could not afford to have the chapel repainted, but neither would they allow any one else to decorate it, lest it should pass out of their hands.

Now another noble family, called the Tournabuoni, when they heard of the fame of the new painter, greatly desired to have a chapel painted by him in order to do honour to their name and family.

Accordingly they went to the Ricci family and offered to have the whole chapel painted and to pay the artist themselves. Moreover, they said that the arms or crest of the Ricci family should be painted in the most honourable part of the chapel, that all might see that the chapel still belonged to them.

To this the Ricci family gladly agreed, and Ghirlandaio was set to work to cover the walls with his frescoes.

`I will give thee twelve hundred gold pieces when it is done,' said Giovanni Tournabuoni, `and if I like it well, then shalt thou have two hundred more.'

Here was good pay indeed. Ghirlandaio set to work with all speed, and day by day the frescoes grew. For four years he worked hard, from morning until night, until at last the walls were covered.

One of the subjects which he chose for these frescoes was the story of the Life of the Virgin, so often painted by Florentine artists. This story I will tell you now, that your eyes may take greater pleasure in the pictures when you see them.

The Bible story of the Virgin Mary begins when the Angel Gabriel came to tell her of the birth of the Baby Jesus, but there are many stories or legends about her before that time, and this is one which the Italians specially loved to paint.

Among the blue hills of Galilee, in the little town of Nazareth, there lived a man and his wife whose names were Joachim and Anna. Though they were rich and had many flocks of sheep which fed in the rich pastures around, still there was one thing which God had not given them and which they longed for more than all beside. They had no child. They had hoped that God would send one, but now they were both growing old, and hope began to fade.

Joachim was a very good man, and gave a third of all that he had as an offering to the temple; but one sad day when he took his gift, the high priest at the altar refused to take it.

`God has shown that He will have nought of thee,' said the priest, `since thou hast no child to come after thee.'

Filled with shame and grief Joachim would not go home to his wife, but instead he wandered out into the far−of fields where his shepherds were feeding the flocks, and there he stayed forty days. With bowed head and sad eyes when he was alone, he knelt and prayed that God would tell him what he had done to deserve this disgrace.

And as he prayed God sent an angel to comfort him.

The angel placed his hand upon the bowed head of the poor old man, and told him to be of good cheer and to return home at once to his wife.

`For God will even now send thee a child,' said the angel.

So with a thankful heart which never doubted the angel's word, Joachim turned his face homewards.

47

Meanwhile, at home, Anna had been sorrowing alone. That same day she had gone into the garden, and, as she wandered among the flowers, she wept bitterly and prayed that God would send her comfort. Then there appeared to her also an angel, who told her that God had heard her prayer and would send her the child she longed for.

`Go now,' the angel added, `and meet thy husband Joachim, who is even now returning to thee, and thou shall find him at the entrance to the Golden Gate.'

So the husband and wife did as the angel bade them, and met together at the Golden Gate. And the Angel of Promise hovered above them, and laid a hand in blessing upon both their heads.

There was no need for speech. As Joachim and Anna looked into each other's eyes and read there the solemn joy of the angel's message, their hearts were filled with peace and comfort.

And before long the angel's promise was fulfilled, and a little daughter was born to Anna and Joachim. In their joy and thankfulness they said she should not be as other children, but should serve in the temple as little Samuel had done. The name they gave the child was Mary, not knowing even then that she was to be the mother of our Lord.

The little maid was but three years old when her parents took her to present her in the temple. She was such a little child that they almost feared she might be frightened to go up the steps to the great temple and meet the high priest alone. So they asked if she might go in company with the other children who were also on their way to the temple. But when the little band arrived at the temple steps, Mary stepped forward and began to climb up, step by step, alone, while the other children and her parents watched wondering from below. Straight up to the temple gates she climbed, and stood with little head bent low to receive the blessing of the great high priest.

So the child was left there to be taught to serve God and to learn how to embroider the purple and fine linen for the priests' vestments. Never before had such exquisite embroidery been done as that which Mary's fingers so delicately stitched, for her work was aided by angel hands. Sleeping or waking, the blessed angels never left her.

When it was time that the maiden should be married, so many suitors came to seek her that it was difficult to know which to choose. To decide the matter they were all told to bring their staves or wands and leave them in the temple all night, that God might show by a sign who was the most worthy to be the guardian of the pure young maid.

Now among the suitors was a poor carpenter of Nazareth called Joseph, who was much older and much poorer than any of the other suitors. They thought it was foolish of him to bring his staff, nevertheless it was placed in the temple with the others.

But when the morning came and the priest went into the temple, behold, Joseph's staff had budded into leaves and flowers, and from among the blossoms there flew out a dove as white as snow.

So it was known that Joseph was to take charge of the young maid, and all the rest of the suitors seized their staves and broke them across their knees in rage and disappointment.

Then the story goes on to the birth of our Saviour as it is told to you in the Bible.

It was this story which Ghirlandaio painted on the walls of the chapel, as well as the history of John the Baptist. Then, as Giovanni directed, he painted the arms of the Tournabuoni on various shields all over the chapel, and only in the tabernacle of the sacrament on the high altar he painted a tiny coat of arms of the Ricci family.

The chapel was finished at last and every one flocked to see it, but first of all came the Ricci, the owners of the chapel.

They looked high and low, but nowhere could they see the arms of their family. Instead, on all sides, they saw the arms of the Tournabuoni. In a great rage they hurried to the Council and demanded that Giovanni Tournabuoni should be punished. But when the facts were explained, and it was shown that the Ricci arms had indeed been placed in the most honourable part, they were obliged to be content, though they vowed vengeance against the Tournabuoni. Neither did Ghirlandaio get his extra two hundred gold pieces, for although Giovanni was delighted with the frescoes he never paid the price he had promised.

To the end of his days Ghirlandaio loved nothing so much as to work from morning till night. Nothing was too small or mean for him to do. He would even paint the hoops for women's baskets rather than send any work away from his shop.

`Oh,' he cried, one day, `how I wish I could paint all the walls around Florence with my stories.'

But there was no time to do all that. He was only forty–four years old when Death came and bade him lay down his brushes and pencil, for his work was done.

Beneath his own frescoes they laid him to rest in the church of Santa Maria Novella. And although we sometimes miss the soul in his pictures and weary of the gay outward decoration of goldsmith's work, yet there is something there which makes us love the grand show of fair ladies and strong men in the carefully finished work of this Florentine `Maker of Garlands.'

FILIPPINO LIPPI

The little curly–haired Filippino, left in the charge of good Fra Diamante, soon showed that he meant to be a painter like his father. When, as a little boy, he drew his pictures and showed them proudly to his mother, he told her that he, too, would learn some day to be a great artist. And she, half smiling, would pat his curly head and tell him that he could at least try his best.

Then, after that sad day when Lucrezia heard of Filippo's death, and the happy little home was broken up, Fra Diamante began in earnest to train the boy who had been left under his care. He had plenty of money, for Filippo had been well paid for the work at Spoleto, and so it was decided that the boy should be placed in some studio where he could be taught all that was necessary.

There was no fear of Filippino ever wandering about the Florentine streets cold and hungry as his father had done. And his training was very different too. Instead of the convent and the kind monks, he was placed under the care of a great painter, and worked in the master's studio with other boys as well off as himself.

The name of Filippino's master was Sandro Botti– celli, a Florentine artist, who had been one of Filippo's pupils and had worked with him in Prato. Fra Diamante knew that he was the greatest artist now in Florence, and that he would be able to teach the child better than any one else.

Filippino was a good, industrious boy, and had none of the faults which had so often led his father into so much mischief and so many strange adventures. His boyhood passed quietly by and he learned all that his master could teach him, and then began to paint his own pictures.

Strangely enough, his first work was to paint the walls of the Carmille Chapel—that same chapel where Filippo and Diamante had learned their lessons, and had gazed with such awe and reverence on Masaccio's work.

The great painter, Ugly Tom, was dead, and there were still parts of the chapel unfinished, so Filippino was invited to fill the empty spaces with his work. No need for the new prior to warn this young painter against the sin of painting earthly pictures. The frescoes which daily grew beneath Filippino's hands were saintly and beautiful. The tall angel in flowing white robes who so gently leads St. Peter out of the prison door, shines with a pure fair light that speaks of Heaven. The sleeping soldier looks in contrast all the more dull and heavy, while St. Peter turns his eyes towards his gentle guide and folds his hands in reverence, wrapped in the soft reflected light of that fair face. And on the opposite wall, the sad face of St. Peter looks out through the prison bars, while a brother saint stands outside, and with uplifted hand speaks comforting words to the poor prisoner.

By slow degrees the chapel walls were finished, and after that there was much work ready for the young painter's hand. It is said that he was very fond of studying old Roman ornaments and painted them into his pictures whenever it was possible, and became very famous for this kind of work. But it is the beauty of his Madonnas and angels that makes us love his pictures, and we like to think that the memory of his gentle mother taught him how to paint those lovely faces.

Perhaps of all his pictures the most beautiful is one in the church of the Badia in Florence. It tells the story of the blessed St. Bernard, and shows the saint in his desert home, as he sat among the rocks writing the history of the Madonna. He had not been able to write that day; perhaps he felt dull, and none of his books, scattered around, were of any help. Then, as he sat lost in thought, with his pen in his hand, the Virgin herself stood before him, an angel on either side, and little angel faces pressed close behind her. Laying a gentle hand upon his book, she seems to tell St. Bernard all those golden words which his poor earthly pen had not been able yet to write.

It used to be the custom long ago in Italy to place in the streets sacred pictures or figures, that passers– by might be reminded of holy things and say a prayer in passing. And still in many towns you will find in some old dusty corner a beautiful picture, painted by a master hand. A gleam of colour will catch your eye, and looking up you see a picture or little shrine of exquisite blue–and–white glazed pottery, where the Madonna kneels and worships the Infant Christ lying amongst the lilies at her feet. The old battered lamp which hangs in front of these shrines is still kept lighted by some faithful hand, and in spring– time the children will often come and lay little bunches of wild–flowers on the ledge below.

`It is for the Jesu Bambino,' they will say, and their little faces grow solemn and reverent as they kneel and say a prayer. Then off again they go to their play.

In a little side–street of Prato, not far from the convent where Filippino's father first saw Lucrezia's lovely face in the sunny garden, there is one of these wayside shrines. It is painted by Filippino, and is one of his most beautiful pictures. The sweet face of the Madonna looks down upon the busy street below, and the Holy Child lifts His little hand in blessing, amid the saints which stand on either side.

The glass that covers the picture is thick with dust, and few who pass ever stop to look up. The world is all too busy nowadays. The hurrying feet pass by, the unseeing eyes grow more and more careless. But Filippino's beautiful Madonna looks on with calm, sad eyes, and the Christ Child, surrounded by the cloud of little angel faces, still holds in His uplifted hand a blessing for those who seek it.

Like all the great Florentine artists, Filippino, as soon as he grew famous, was invited to Rome, and he painted many pictures there. On his way he stopped for a while at Spoleto, and there he designed a beautiful marble monument for his father's tomb.

Unlike that father, Filippino was never fond of travel or adventure, and was always glad to return to Florence and live his quiet life there. Not even an invitation from the King of

Hungary could tempt him to leave home.

It was in the great church of Santa Maria Novella in Florence that Filippino painted his last frescoes. They are very real and lifelike, as one of the great painter's pupils once learned to his cost. Filippino had, of course, many pupils who worked under him. They ground his colours and watched him work, and would sometimes be allowed to prepare the less important parts of the picture.

Now it happened that one day when the master had finished his work and had left the chapel, that one of the pupils lingered behind. His sharp eye had caught sight of a netted purse which lay in a dark corner, dropped there by some careless visitor, or perhaps by the master himself. The boy darted back and caught up the treasure; but at that moment the master turned back to fetch something he had forgotten. The boy looked quickly round. Where could he hide his prize? In a moment his eye fell on a hole in the wall, underneath a step which Filippino had been painting in the fresco. That was the very place, and he ran forward to thrust the purse inside. But, alas! the hole was only a painted one, and the boy was fairly caught, and was obliged with shame and confusion to give up his prize.

Scarcely were these frescoes finished when Filippino was seized with a terrible fever, and he died almost as suddenly as his father had done.

In those days when there was a funeral of a prince in Florence, the Florentines used to shut their shops, and this was considered a great mark of respect, and was paid only to those of royal blood. But on the day that Filippino's funeral passed along the Via dei Servi, every shop there was closed and all Florence mourned for him.

`Some men,' they said, `are born princes, and some raise themselves by their talents to be kings among men. Our Filippino was a prince in Art, and so do we do honour to his title.'

PIETRO PERUGINO

It was early morning, and the rays of the rising sun had scarcely yet caught the roofs of the city of Perugia, when along the winding road which led across the plain a man and a boy walked with steady, purposelike steps towards the town which crowned the hill in front.

The man was poorly dressed in the common rough clothes of an Umbrian peasant. Hard work and poverty had bent his shoulders and drawn stern lines upon his face, but there was a dignity about him which marked him as something above the common working man.

The little boy who trotted barefoot along by the side of his father had a sweet, serious little face, but he looked tired and hungry, and scarcely fit for such a long rough walk. They had started from their home at Castello delle Pieve very early that morning, and the piece of black bread which had served them for breakfast had been but small. Away in front stretched that long, white, never–ending road; and the little dusty feet that pattered so bravely along had to take hurried runs now and again to keep up with the long strides of the man, while the wistful eyes, which were fixed on that distant town, seemed to wonder if they would really ever reach their journey's end.

`Art tired already, Pietro?' asked the father at length, hearing a panting little sigh at his side. `Why, we are not yet half–way there! Thou must step bravely out and be a man, for to–day thou shalt begin to work for thy living, and no longer live the life of an idle child.'

The boy squared his shoulders, and his eyes shone.

`It is not I who am tired, my father,' he said. `It is only that my legs cannot take such good long steps as thine; and walk as we will the road ever seems to unwind itself further and further in front, like the magic white thread which has no end.'

The father laughed, and patted the child's head kindly.

`The end will come ere long,' he said. `See where the mist lies at the foot of the hill; there we will begin to climb among the olive–trees and leave the dusty road. I know a quicker way by which we may reach the city. We will climb over the great stones that mark the track of the stream, and before the sun grows too hot we will have reached the city gates.'

It was a great relief to the little hot, tired feet to feel the cool grass beneath them, and to leave the dusty road. The boy almost forgot his tiredness as he scrambled from stone to stone, and filled his hands with the violets which grew thickly on the banks, scenting the morning air with their sweetness. And when at last they came out once more upon the great white road before the city gates, there was so much to gaze upon and wonder at, that there was no room for thoughts of weariness or hunger.

There stood the herds of great white oxen, patiently waiting to pass in. Pietro wondered if their huge wide horns would not reach from side to side of the narrow street within the gates. There the shepherd–boys played sweet airs upon their pipes as they walked before their flocks, and led the silly frightened sheep out of the way of passing carts. Women with bright–coloured handkerchiefs tied over their heads crowded round, carrying baskets of fruit and vegetables from the country round. Carts full of scarlet and yellow pumpkins were driven noisily along. Whips cracked, people shouted and talked as much with their hands as with their lips, and all were eager to pass through the great Etruscan gateway, which stood grim and tall against the blue of the summer sky. Much good service had that gateway seen, and it was as strong as when it had been first built hundreds of years before, and was still able to shut out an army of enemies, if Perugia had need to defend herself.

Pietro and his father quickly threaded their way through the crowd, and passed through the gateway into the steep narrow street beyond. It was cool and quiet here. The sun was shut out by the tall houses, and the shadows lay so deep that one might have thought it was the hour of twilight, but for the peep of bright blue sky which showed between the overhanging eaves above. Presently they reached the great square market–place, where all again was sunshine and bustle, with people shouting and selling their wares, which they spread out on the ground up to the very steps of the cathedral and all along in front of the Palazzo Publico. Here the man stopped, and asked one of the passers–by if he could direct him to the shop of Niccolo the painter.

`Yonder he dwells,' answered the citizen, and pointed to a humble shop at the corner of the market–place. `Hast thou brought the child to be a model?'

Pietro held his head up proudly, and answered quickly for himself.

`I am no longer a child,' he said; `and I have come to work and not to sit idle.'

The man laughed and went his way, while father and son hurried on towards the little shop and entered the door.

The old painter was busy, and they had to wait a while until he could leave his work and come to see what they might want.

`This is the boy of whom I spoke,' said the father as he pushed Pietro forward by his shoulder. `He is not well grown, but he is strong, and has learnt to endure hardness. I promise thee that he will serve thee well if thou wilt take him as thy servant.'

The painter smiled down at the little eager face which was waiting so anxiously for his answer.

`What canst thou do?' he asked the boy.

`Everything,' answered Pietro promptly. `I can sweep out thy shop and cook thy dinner. I will learn to grind thy colours and wash thy brushes, and do a man's work.'

`In faith,' laughed the painter, `if thou canst do everything, being yet so young, thou wilt soon be the greatest man in Perugia, and bring great fame to this fair city. Then will we call thee no longer Pietro Vanucci, but thou shalt take the city's name, and we will call thee Perugino.'

The master spoke in jest, but as time went on and he watched the boy at work, he marvelled at the quickness with which the child learned to perform his new duties, and began to think the jest might one day turn to earnest.

From early morning until sundown Pietro was never idle, and when the rough work was done he would stand and watch the master as he painted, and listen breathless to the tales which Niccolo loved to tell.

`There is nothing so great in all the world as the art of painting,' the master would say. `It is the ladder that leads up to heaven, the window which lets light into the soul. A painter need never be lonely or poor. He can create the faces he loves, while all the riches of light and colour and beauty are always his. If thou hast it in thee to be a painter, my little Perugino, I can wish thee no greater fortune.'

Then when the day's work was done and the short spell of twilight drew near, the boy would leave the shop and run swiftly down the narrow street until he came to the grim old city gates. Once outside, under the wide blue sky in the free open air of the country, he drew a long, long breath of pleasure, and quickly found a hidden corner in the cleft of the hoary trunk of an olive–tree, where no passer–by could see him. There he sat, his chin resting on his hands, gazing and gazing out over the plain below, drinking in the beauty with his hungry eyes.

How he loved that great open space of sweet fresh air, in the calm pure light of the evening hour. That white light, which seemed to belong more to heaven than to earth, shone on everything around. Away in the distance the purple hills faded into the sunset sky. At his feet the plain stretched away, away until it met the mountains, here and there lifting itself in some little hill crowned by a lonely town whose roofs just caught the rays of the setting sun. The evening mist lay like a gossamer veil upon the low–lying lands, and between the little towns the long straight road could be seen, winding like a white ribbon through the grey and silver, and marked here and there by a dark cypress–tree or a tall poplar. And always there would be a glint of blue, where a stream or river caught the reflection of the sky and held it lovingly there, like a mirror among the rocks.

But Pietro did not have much time for idle dreaming. His was not an easy life, for Niccolo made but little money with his painting, and the boy had to do all the work of the house besides attending to the shop. But all the time he was sweeping and dusting he looked forward to the happy days to come when he might paint pictures and become a famous artist.

Whenever a visitor came to the shop, Pietro would listen eagerly to his talk and try to learn something of the great world of Art. Sometimes he would even venture to ask questions, if the stranger happened to be one who had travelled from afar.

`Where are the most beautiful pictures to be found?' he asked one day when a Florentine painter had come to the little shop and had been describing the glories he had seen in other cities. `And where is it that the greatest painters dwell?'

`That is an easy question to answer, my boy,' said the painter. `All that is fairest is to be found in Florence, the most beautiful city in all the world, the City of Flowers. There one may find the best of everything, but above all, the most beautiful pictures and the greatest of painters. For no one there can bear to do only the second best, and a man must attain to the very highest before the Florentines will call him great. The walls of the churches and monasteries are covered with pictures of saints and angels, and their beauty no words can describe.'

`I too will go to Florence, said Pietro to himself, and every day he longed more and more to see that wonderful city.

It was no use to wait until he should have saved enough money to take him there. He scarcely earned enough to live on from day to day. So at last, poor as he was, he started off early one morning and said good–bye to his old master and the hard work of the little shop in Perugia. On he went down the same long white road which had seemed so endless to him that day when, as a little child, he first came to Perugia. Even now, when he was a strong young man, the way seemed long and weary across that great plain, and he was often foot– sore and discouraged. Day after day he travelled on, past the great lake which lay like a sapphire in the bosom of the plain, past many towns and little villages, until at last he came in sight of the City of Flowers.

It was a wonderful moment to Perugino, and he held his breath as he looked. He had passed the brow of the hill, and stood beside a little stream bordered by a row of tall, straight poplars which showed silvery white against the blue sky. Beyond, nestling at the foot of the encircling hills, lay the city of his dreams. Towers and palaces, a crowding together of pale red sunbaked roofs, with the great dome of the cathedral in the midst, and the silver thread of the Arno winding its way between—all this he saw, but he saw more than this. For it seemed to him that the Spirit of Beauty hovered above the fair city, and he almost heard the rustle of her wings and caught a glimpse of her rainbow–tinted robe in the light of the evening sky.

Poor Pietro! Here was the world he longed to conquer, but he was only a poor country boy, and how was he to begin to climb that golden ladder of Art which led men to fame and glory?

Well, he could work, and that was always a beginning. The struggle was hard, and for many a month he often went hungry and had not even a bed to lie on at night, but curled himself up on a hard wooden chest. Then good fortune began to smile upon him.

The Florentine artists to whose studios he went began to notice the hardworking boy, and when they looked at his work, with all its faults and want of finish, they saw in it that divine something called genius which no one can mistake.

Then the doors of another world seemed to open to Pietro. All day long he could now work at his beloved painting and learn fresh wonders as he watched the great men use the brush and pencil. In the studio of the painter Verocchio he met the men of whose fame he had so often heard, and whose work he looked upon with awe and reverence.

There was the good—tempered monk of the Carmine, Fra Filipo Lippi, the young Botticelli, and a youth just his own age whom they called Leonardo da Vinci, of whom it was whispered already that he would some day be the greatest master of the age.

These were golden days for Perugino, as he was called, for the name of the city where he had come from was always now given to him. The pictures he had longed to paint grew beneath his hand, and upon his canvas began to dawn the solemn dignity and open—air spaciousness of those evening visions he had seen when he gazed across the Umbrian Plain. There was no noise of battle, no human passion in his pictures. His saints stood quiet and solemn, single figures with just a thread of interest binding them together, and always beyond was the great wide open world, with the white light shining in the sky, the blue thread of the river, and the single trees pointing upwards—dark, solemn cypress, or feathery larch or poplar.

There was much for the young painter still to learn, and perhaps he learned most from the silent teaching of that little dark chapel of the Carmine, where Masaccio taught more wonderful lessons by his frescoes than any living artist could teach.

Then came the crowning honour when Perugino received an invitation from the Pope to go to Rome and paint the walls of the Sistine Chapel. Hence forth it was a different kind of life for the young painter. No need to wonder where he would get his next meal, no hard rough wooden chest on which to rest his weary limbs when the day's work was done. Now he was royally entertained and softly lodged, and men counted it an honour to be in his company.

But though he loved Florence and was proud to do his painting in Rome, his heart ever drew him back to the city on the hill whose name he bore.

Again he travelled along the winding road, and his heart beat fast as he drew nearer and saw the familiar towers and roofs of Perugia. How well he remembered that long—ago day when the cool touch of the grass was so grateful to his little tired dusty feet! He stooped again to fill his hands with the sweet violets, and thought them sweeter than all the fame and fair show of the gay cities.

And as he passed through the ancient gateway and threaded his way up the narrow street towards the little shop, he seemed to see once more the kindly smile of his old master and to hear him say, `Thou wilt soon be the greatest man in Perugia, and we will call thee no longer Pietro Vanucci, but Perugino.'

So it had come to pass. Here he was. No longer a little ragged, hungry boy, but a man whom all delighted to honour. Truly this was a world of changes!

A bigger studio was needed than the little old shop, for now he had more pictures to paint than he well knew how to finish. Then, too, he had many pupils, for all were eager to enter the studio of the great master. There it was that one morning a new pupil was brought to him, a boy of twelve, whose guardians begged that Perugino would teach and train him.

Perugino looked with interest at the child. Seldom had he seen such a beautiful oval face, framed by such soft brown curls—a face so pure and lovable that even at first sight it drew out love from the hearts of those who looked at him.

`His father was also a painter,' said the guardian, `and Raphael, here, has caught the trick of using his pencil and brush, so we would have him learn of the greatest master in the land.'

After some talk, the boy was left in the studio at Perugia, and day by day Perugino grew to love him more. It was not only that little Raphael was clever and skilful, though that alone often made the master marvel.

`He is my pupil now, but some day he will be my master, and I shall learn of him,' Perugino would often say as he watched the boy at work. But more than all, the pure sweet nature and the polished gentleness of his manners charmed the heart of the master, and he loved to have the boy always near him, and to teach him was his greatest pleasure.

Knights of the Art: Stories

Those quiet days in the Perugia studio never lasted very long. From all quarters came calls to Perugino, and, much as he loved work, he could not finish all that was wanted.

It happened once when he was in Florence that a certain prior begged him to come and fresco the walls of his convent. This prior was very famous for making a most beautiful and expensive blue colour which he was anxious should be used in the painting of the convent walls. He was a mean, suspicious man, and would not trust Perugino with the precious blue colour, but always held it in his own hands and grudgingly doled it out in small quantities, torn between the desire to have the colour on his walls and his dislike to parting with anything so precious.

As Perugino noted this, he grew angry and determined to punish the prior's meanness. The next time therefore that there was a blue sky to be painted, he put at his side a large bowl of fresh water, and then called on the prior to put out a small quantity of the blue colour in a little vase. Each time he dipped his brush into the vase, Perugino washed it out with a swirl in the bowl at his side, so that most of the colour was left in the water, and very little was put on to the picture.

`I pray thee fill the vase again with blue,' he said carelessly when the colour was all gone. The prior groaned aloud, and turned grudgingly to his little bag.

`Oh what a quantity of blue is swallowed up by this plaster!' he said, as he gazed at the white wall, which scarcely showed a trace of the precious colour.

`Yes,' said Perugino cheerfully, `thou canst see thyself how it goes.'

Then afterwards, when the prior had sadly gone off with his little empty bag, Perugino carefully poured the water from the bowl and gathered together the grains of colour which had sunk to the bottom.

`Here is something that belongs to thee,' he said sternly to the astonished prior. `I would have thee learn to trust honest men and not treat them as thieves. For with all thy suspicious care, it was easy to rob thee if I had had a mind.'

During all these years in which Perugino had worked so diligently, the art of painting had been growing rapidly. Many of the new artists shook off the old rules and ideas, and began to paint in quite a new way. There was one man especially, called Michelangelo, whose story you will hear later on, who arose like a giant, and with his new way and greater knowledge swept everything before him.

Perugino was jealous of all these new ideas, and clung more closely than ever to his old ideals, his quiet, dignified saints, and spacious landscapes. He talked openly of his dislike of the new style, and once he had a serious quarrel with the great Michelangelo.

There was a gathering of painters in Perugino's studio that day. Filippino Lippi, Botticelli, Ghirlandaio, and Leonardo were there, and in the background the pupil Raphael was listening to the talk.

`What dost thou think of this new style of painting?' asked Botticelli. `To me it seems but strange and unpleasing. Music and motion are delightful, but this violent twisting of limbs to show the muscles offends my taste.'

`Yet it is most marvellously skilful,' said the young Leonardo thoughtfully.

`But totally unfit for the proper picturing of saints and the blessed Madonna,' said Filippino, shaking his curly head.

`I never trouble myself about it,' said Ghirlandaio. `Life is too short to attend to other men's work. It takes all my care and attention to look after mine own. But see, here comes the great Michelangelo himself to listen to our criticism.'

The curious, rugged face of the great artist looked good–naturedly on the company, but his strong knotted hands waved aside their greetings.

`So you were busy as usual finding fault with my work,' he said. `Come, friend Perugino, tell me what thou hast found to grumble at.'

`I like not thy methods, and that I tell thee frankly,' answered Perugino, an angry light shining in his eyes. `It is such work as thine that drags the art of painting down from the heights of heavenly things to the low taste of earth. It robs it of all dignity and restfulness, and destroys the precious traditions handed down to us since the days of Giotto.'

The face of Michelangelo grew angry and scornful as he listened to this.

`Thou art but a dolt and a blockhead in Art,' he said. `Thou wilt soon see that the day of thy saints and Madonnas is past, and wilt cease to paint them over and over again in the same manner, as a child doth his lesson in a copy book.'

Then he turned and went out of the studio before any one had time to answer him.

Perugino was furiously angry and would not listen to reason, but must needs go before the great Council and demand that they should punish Michelangelo for his hard words. This of course the Council refused to do, and Perugino left Florence for Perugia, angry and sore at heart.

It seemed hard, after all his struggles and great successes, that as he grew old people should begin to tire of his work, which they had once thought so perfect.

But if the outside world was sometimes disappointing, he had always his home to turn to, and his beautiful wife Chiare. He had married her in his beloved Perugia, and she meant all the joy of life to him. He was so proud of her beauty that he would buy her the richest dresses and most costly jewels, and with his own hands would deck her with them. Her brown eyes were like the depths of some quiet pool, her fair face and the wonderful soul that shone there were to him the most perfect picture in the world.

`I will paint thee once, that the world may be the richer,' said Perugino, `but only once, for thy beauty is too rare for common use. And I will paint thee not as an earthly beauty, but thou shalt be the angel in the story of Tobias which thou knowest.'

So he painted her as he said. And in our own National Gallery we still have the picture, and we may see her there as the beautiful angel who leads the little boy Tobias by the hand.

Up to the very last years of his life, Perugino painted as diligently as he had ever done, but the peaceful days of Perugia had long since given place to war and tumult, both within and without the city. Then too a terrible plague swept over the countryside, and people died by thousands.

To the hospital of Fartignano, close to Perugia, they carried Perugino when the deadly plague seized him, and there he died. There was no time to think of grand funerals; the people were buried as quickly as possible, in whatever place lay closest at hand.

So it came to pass that Perugino was laid to rest in an open field under an oak–tree close by. Later on his sons wished to have him buried in holy ground, and some say that this was done, but nothing is known for certain. Perhaps if he could have chosen, he would have been glad to think that his body should rest under the shelter of the trees he loved to paint, in that waste openness of space which had always been his vision of beauty, since, as a little boy, he gazed across the Umbrian Plain, and the wonder of it sank into his soul.

LEONARDO DA VINCI

On the sunny slopes of Monte Albano, between Florence and Pisa, the little town of Vinci lay high among the rocks that crowned the steep hillside. It was but a little town. Only a few houses crowded together round an old castle in the midst, and it looked from a distance like a swallow's nest clinging to the bare steep rocks.

Here in the year 1452 Leonardo, son of Ser Piero da Vinci, was born. It was in the age when people told fortunes by the stars, and when a baby was born they would eagerly look up and decide whether it was a lucky or unlucky star which shone upon the child. Surely if it had been possible in this way to tell what fortune awaited the little Leonardo, a strange new star must have shone that night, brighter than the others and unlike the rest in the dazzling light of its strength and beauty.

Leonardo was always a strange child. Even his beauty was not like that of other children. He had the most wonderful waving hair, falling in regular ripples, like the waters of a fountain, the colour of bright gold, and soft as spun silk. His eyes were blue and clear, with a mysterious light in them, not the warm light of a sunny sky, but rather the blue that glints in the iceberg. They were merry eyes too, when he laughed, but underneath was always that strange cold look. There was a charm about his smile which no one could resist, and he was a favourite with all. Yet people shook their heads sometimes as they looked at him, and they talked in whispers of the old witch who had lent her goat to nourish the little Leonardo when he was a baby. The woman was a dealer in black magic, and who knew but that the child might be a changeling?

Knights of the Art: Stories

It was the old grandmother, Mona Lena, who brought Leonardo up and spoilt him not a little. His father, Ser Piero, was a lawyer, and spent most of his time in Florence, but when he returned to the old castle of Vinci, he began to give Leonardo lessons and tried to find out what the boy was fit for. But Leonardo hated those lessons and would not learn, so when he was seven years old he was sent to school.

This did not answer any better. The rough play of the boys was not to his liking. When he saw them drag the wings off butterflies, or torture any animal that fell into their hands, his face grew white with pain, and he would take no share in their games. The Latin grammar, too, was a terrible task, while the many things he longed to know no one taught him.

So it happened that many a time, instead of going to school, he would slip away and escape up into the hills, as happy as a little wild goat. Here was all the sweet fresh air of heaven, instead of the stuffy schoolroom. Here were no cruel, clumsy boys, but all the wild creatures that he loved. Here he could learn the real things his heart was hungry to know, not merely words which meant nothing and led to nowhere.

For hours he would lie perfectly still with his heels in the air and his chin resting in his hands, as he watched a spider weaving its web, breathless with interest to see how the delicate threads were turned in and out. The gaily painted butterflies, the fat buzzing bees, the little sharp–tongued green lizards, he loved to watch them all, but above everything he loved the birds. Oh, if only he too had wings to dart like the swallows, and swoop and sail and dart again! What was the secret power in their wings? Surely by watching he might learn it. Sometimes it seemed as if his heart would burst with the longing to learn that secret. It was always the hidden reason of things that he desired to know. Much as he loved the flowers he must pull their petals of, one by one, to see how each was joined, to wonder at the dusty pollen, and touch the honey–covered stamens. Then when the sun began to sink he would turn sadly homewards, very hungry, with torn clothes and tired feet, but with a store of sunshine in his heart.

His grandmother shook her head when Leonardo appeared after one of his days of wandering.

`I know thou shouldst be whipped for playing truant,' she said; `and I should also punish thee for tearing thy clothes.'

`Ah! but thou wilt not whip me,' answered Leonardo, smiling at her with his curious quiet smile, for he had full confidence in her love.

`Well, I love to see thee happy, and I will not punish thee this time,' said his grandmother; `but if these tales reach thy father's ears, he will not be so tender as I am towards thee.'

And, sure enough, the very next time that a complaint was made from the school, his father happened to be at home, and then the storm burst.

`Next time I will flog thee,' said Ser Piero sternly, with rising anger at the careless air of the boy. `Meanwhile we will see what a little imprisonment will do towards making thee a better child.'

Then he took the boy by the shoulders and led him to a little dark cupboard under the stairs, and there shut him up for three whole days.

There was no kicking or beating at the locked door. Leonardo sat quietly there in the dark, thinking his own thoughts, and wondering why there seemed so little justice in the world. But soon even that wonder passed away, and as usual when he was alone he began to dream dreams of the time when he should have learned the swallows' secrets and should have wings like theirs.

But if there were complaints about Leonardo's dislike of the boys and the Latin grammar, there would be none about the lessons he chose to learn. Indeed, some of the masters began to dread the boy's eager questions, which were sometimes more than they could answer. Scarcely had he begun the study of arithmetic than he made such rapid progress, and wanted to puzzle out so many problems, that the masters were amazed. His mind seemed always eagerly asking for more light, and was never satisfied.

But it was out on the hillside that he spent his happiest hours. He loved every crawling, creeping, or flying thing, however ugly. Curious beasts which might have frightened another child were to him charming and interesting. There as he listened to the carolling of the birds and bent his head to catch the murmured song of the mountain—streams, the love of music began to steal into his heart.

He did not rest then until he managed to get a lute and learned how to play upon it. And when he had mastered the notes and learned the rules of music, he began to play airs which no one had ever heard before, and to sing such strange sweet songs that the golden notes flowed out as fresh and clear as the song of a lark in the early morning of spring.

`The child is a changeling,' said some, as they saw Leonardo tenderly lift a crushed lizard in his hand, or watched him play with a spotted snake or great hairy spider.

`A changeling perhaps,' said others, `but one that hath the voice of an angel.' For every one stopped to listen when the boy's voice was heard singing through the streets of the little town.

He was a puzzle to every one, and yet a delight to all, even when they understood him least.

So time went on, and when Leonardo was thirteen his father took him away to Florence that he might begin to be trained for some special work. But what work? Ah! that was the rub. The boy could do so many things well that it was difficult to fix on one.

At that time there was living in Florence an old man who knew a great deal about the stars, and who made wonderful calculations about them. He was a famous astronomer, but he cared not at all for honour or fame, but lived a simple quiet life by himself and would not mix with the gay world.

Few visitors ever came to see him, for it was known that he would receive no one, and so it was a great surprise to old Toscanelli when one night a gentle knock sounded at his door, and a boy walked quietly in and stood before him.

Hastily the old man looked up, and his first thought was to ask the child how he dared enter without leave, and then ask him to be gone, but as he looked at the fair face he felt the charm of the curious smile, and the light in the blue eyes, and instead he laid his hand upon the boy's golden head and said: `What dost thou seek, my son?'

`I would learn all that thou canst teach me,' said Leonardo, for it was he.

The old man smiled.

`Behold the boundless self-confidence of youth!' he said.

But as they talked together, and the boy asked his many eager questions, a great wonder awoke in the astronomer's mind, and his eyes shone with interest. This child-mind held depths of understanding such as he had never met with among his learned friends. Day after day the old man and the boy bent eagerly together over their problems, and when night fell Toscanelli would take the child up with him to his lonely tower above Florence, and teach him to know the stars and to understand many things.

`This is all very well,' said Ser Piero, `but the boy must do more than mere star-gazing. He must earn a living for himself, and methinks we might make a painter of him.'

That very day, therefore, he gathered together some of Leonardo's drawings which lay carelessly scattered about, and took them to the studio of Verocchio the painter, who lived close by the Ponte Vecchio.

`Dost thou think thou canst make aught of the boy?' he asked, spreading out the drawings before Verocchio.

The painter's quick eyes examined the work with deep interest.

`Send him to me at once,' he said. `This is indeed marvellous talent.'

So Leonardo entered the studio as a pupil, and learned all that could be taught him with the same quickness with which he learned anything that he cared to know.

Every one who saw his work declared that he would be the wonder of the age, but Verocchio shook his head.

`He is too wonderful,' he said. `He aims at too great perfection. He wants to know everything and do everything, and life is too short for that. He finishes nothing, because he is ever starting to do something else.'

Verocchio's words were true; the boy seldom worked long at one thing. His hands were never idle, and often, instead of painting, he would carve out tiny windmills and curious toys which worked with pulleys and ropes, or made exquisite little clay models of horses and all the other animals that he loved. But he never forgot the longing that had filled his heart when he was a child—the desire to learn the secret of flying.

For days he would sit idle and think of nothing but soaring wings, then he would rouse himself and begin to make some strange machine which he thought might hold the secret that he sought.

`A waste of time,' growled Verocchio. `See here, thou wouldst be better employed if thou shouldst set to work and help me finish this picture of the Baptism for the good monks of Vallambrosa. Let me see how thou canst paint in the kneeling figure of the angel at the side.'

For a while the boy stood motionless before the picture as if he was looking at something far away. Then he seized the brushes with his left hand and began to paint with quick certain sweep. He never stopped to think, but worked as if the angel were already there, and he were but brushing away the veil that hid it from the light.

Then, when it was done, the master came and looked silently on. For a moment a quick stab of jealousy ran through his heart. Year after year had he worked and striven to reach his ideal. Long days of toil and weary nights had he spent, winning each step upwards by sheer hard work. And here was this boy without an effort able to rise far above him. All the knowledge which the master had groped after, had been grasped at once by the wonderful mind of the pupil. But the envious feeling passed quickly away, and Verocchio laid his hand upon Leonardo's shoulder.

`I have found my master,' he said quietly, `and I will paint no more.'

Leonardo scarcely seemed to hear; he was thinking of something else now, and he seldom noticed if people praised or blamed him. His thoughts had fixed themselves upon something he had seen that morning which had troubled him. On the way to the studio he had passed a tiny shop in a narrow street where a seller of birds was busy hanging his cages up on the nails fastened to the outside wall.

The thought of those poor little prisoners beating their wings against the cruel bars and breaking their hearts with longing for their wild free life, had haunted him all day, and now he could bear it no longer. He seized his cap and hurried off, all forgetful of his kneeling angel and the master's praise.

He reached the little shop and called to the man within.

`How much wilt thou take for thy birds?' he cried, and pointed to the little wooden cages that hung against the wall.

`Plague on them,' answered the man, `they will often die before I can make a sale by them. Thou canst have them all for one silver piece.'

In a moment Leonardo had paid the money and had turned towards the row of little cages. One by one he opened the doors and set the prisoners free, and those that were too frightened or timid to fly away, he gently drew out with his hand, and sent them gaily whirling up above his head into the blue sky.

The man looked with blank astonishment at the empty cages, and wondered if the handsome young man was mad. But Leonardo paid no heed to him, but stood gazing up until every one of the birds had disappeared.

`Happy things,' he said, with a sigh. `Will you ever teach me the secret of your wings, I wonder?'

It was with great pleasure that Ser Piero heard of his son's success at Verocchio's studio, and he began to have hopes that the boy would make a name for himself after all. It happened just then that he was on a visit to his castle at Vinci, and one morning a peasant who lived on the estate came to ask a great favour of him.

He had bought a rough wooden shield which he was very anxious should have a design painted on it in Florence, and he begged Ser Piero to see that it was done. The peasant was a faithful servant, and very useful in supplying the castle with fish and game, so Ser Piero was pleased to grant him his request.

`Leonardo shall try his hand upon it. It is time he became useful to me,' said Ser Piero to himself. So on his return to Florence he took the shield to his son.

It was a rough, badly–shaped shield, so Leonardo held it to the fire and began to straighten it. For though his hands looked delicate and beautifully formed, they were as strong as steel, and he could bend bars of iron without an effort. Then he sent the shield to a turner to be smoothed and rounded, and when it was ready he sat down to think what he should paint upon it, for he loved to draw strange monsters.

`I will make it as terrifying as the head of Medusa,' he said at last, highly delighted with the plan that had come into his head.

Then he went out and collected together all the strangest animals he could find—lizards, hedgehogs, newts, snakes, dragon–flies, locusts, bats, and glow– worms. These he took into his own room, which no one was allowed to enter, and began to paint from them a curious monster, partly a lizard and partly a bat, with something of each of the other animals added to it.

When it was ready Leonardo hung the shield in a good light against a dark curtain, so that the painted monster stood out in brilliant contrast, and looked as if its twisted curling limbs were full of life.

A knock sounded at the door, and Ser Piero's voice was heard outside asking if the shield was finished.

`Come in,' cried Leonardo, and Ser Piero entered.

He cast one look at the monster hanging there and then uttered a cry and turned to flee, but Leonardo caught hold of his cloak and laughingly told him to look closer.

`If I have really succeeded in frightening thee,' he said, `I have indeed done all I could desire.'

His father could scarcely believe that it was nothing but a painting, and he was so proud of the work that he would not part with it, but gave the peasant of Vinci another shield instead.

Leonardo then began a drawing for a curtain which was to be woven in silk and gold and given as a present from the Florentines to the King of Portugal, and he also began a large picture of the Adoration of the Shepherds which was never finished.

The young painter grew restless after a while, and felt the life of the studio narrow and cramped. He longed to leave Florence and find work in some new place.

He was not a favourite at the court of Lorenzo the Magnificent as Filippino Lippi and Botticelli were. Lorenzo liked those who would flatter him and do as they were bid, while Leonardo took his own way in everything and never said what he did not mean.

But it happened that just then Lorenzo wished to send a present to Ludovico Sforza, the Duke of Milan, and the gift he chose was a marvellous musical instrument which Leonardo had just finished.

It was a silver lute, made in the form of a horse's head, the most curious and beautiful thing ever seen. Lorenzo was charmed with it.

`Thou shalt take it thyself, as my messenger,' he said to Leonardo. `I doubt if another can be found who can play upon it as thou dost.'

So Leonardo set out for Milan, and was glad to shake himself free from the narrow life of the Florentine studio.

Before starting, however, he had written a letter to the Duke setting down in simple order all the things he could do, and telling of what use he could be in times of war and in days of peace.

There seemed nothing that he could not do. He could make bridges, blow up castles, dig canals, invent a new kind of cannon, build warships, and make underground passages. In days of peace he could design and build houses, make beautiful statues and paint pictures `as well as any man, be he who he may.'

The letter was written in curious writing from right to left like Hebrew or Arabic. This was how Leonardo always wrote, using his left hand, so that it could only be read by holding the writing up to a mirror.

The Duke was half amazed and half amused when the letter reached him.

`Either these are the words of a fool, or of a man of genius,' said the Duke. And when he had once seen and spoken to Leonardo he saw at once which of the two he deserved to be called.

Every one at the court was charmed with the artist's beautiful face and graceful manners. His music alone, as he swept the strings of the silver lute and sang to it his own songs, would have brought him fame, but the Duke quickly saw that this was no mere minstrel.

It was soon arranged therefore that Leonardo should take up his abode at the court of Milan and receive a yearly pension from the Duke.

Sometimes the pension was paid, and sometimes it was forgotten, but Leonardo never troubled about money matters. Somehow or other he must have all that he wanted, and everything must be fair and dainty. His clothes were always rich and costly, but never bright–coloured or gaudy. There was no plume or jewelled brooch in his black velvet beretto or cap, and the only touch of colour was his golden hair, and the mantle of dark red cloth which he wore in the fashion of the Florentines, thrown across his shoulder. Above all, he must always have horses in his stables, for he loved them more than human beings.

Many were the plans and projects which the Duke entrusted to Leonardo's care, but of all that he did, two great works stand out as greater than all the rest. One was the painting of the Last Supper on the walls of the refectory of Santa Maria delle Grazie, and the other the making of a model of a great equestrian statue, a bronze horse with the figure of the Duke upon its back.

`Year after year Leonardo worked at that wonderful fresco of the Last Supper. Sometimes for weeks or months he never touched it, but he always returned to it again. Then for days he would work from morning till night, scarcely taking time to eat, and able to think of nothing else, until suddenly he would put down his brushes and stand silently for a long, long time before the picture. It seemed as if he was wasting the precious hours doing nothing, but in truth he worked more diligently with his brain when his hands were idle.

Often too when he worked at the model for the great bronze horse, he would suddenly stop, and walk quickly through the streets until he came to the refectory, and there, catching up his brushes, he would paint in one or perhaps two strokes, and then return to his modelling.

Besides all this Leonardo was busy with other plans for the Duke's amusement, and no court fete was counted successful without his help. Nothing seemed too difficult for him to contrive, and what he did was always new and strange and wonderful.

Once when the King of France came as a guest to Milan, Leonardo prepared a curious model of a lion, which by some inside machinery was able to walk forward several steps to meet the King, and then open wide its huge jaws and display inside a bed of sweet–scented lilies, the emblem of France, to do honour to her King. But while working at other things Leonardo never forgot his longing to learn the secret art of flying. Every now and then a new idea would come into his head, and he would lay aside all other work until he had made the new machine which might perhaps act as the wings of a bird. Each fresh disappointment only made him more keen to try again.

`I know we shall some day have wings,' he said to his pupils, who sometimes wondered at the strange work of the master's hands. `It is only a question of knowing how to make them. I remember once when I was a baby lying in my cradle, I fancied a bird flew to me, opened my lips and rubbed its feathers over them. So it seems to be my fate all my life to talk of wings.'

Very slowly the great fresco of the Last Supper grew under the master's hand until it was nearly finished. The statue, too, was almost completed, and then evil days fell upon Milan. The Duke was obliged to flee before the French soldiers, who forced their way into the town and took possession of it. Before any one could prevent it, the soldiers began to shoot their arrows at the great statue, which they used as a target, and in a few hours the work of sixteen years was utterly destroyed. It is sadder still to tell the fate of Leonardo's fresco, the greatest picture perhaps that ever was painted. Dampness lurked in the wall and began to dim and blur the colours. The careless monks cut a door through the very centre of the picture, and, later on, when Napoleon's soldiers entered Milan, they used the refectory as a stable, and amused themselves by throwing stones at what remained of it. But though little of it is left now to be seen, there is still enough to make us stand in awe and reverence before the genius of the great master.

Not far from Milan there lived a friend of Leonardo's, whom the master loved to visit. This Girolamo Melzi had a son called Francesco, a little motherless boy, who adored the great painter with all his heart.

Together Leonardo and the child used to wander out to search for curious animals and rare flowers, and as they watched the spiders weave their webs and pulled the flowers to pieces to find out their secrets, the boy listened with wide wondering eyes to all the tales which the painter told him. And at night Leonardo wrapped the little one close inside his warm cloak and carried him out to see the stars—those same stars which old Toscanelli had taught him to love long ago in Florence. Then when the day of parting came the child clung round the master's neck and would not let him go.

`Take me with thee,' he cried, `do not leave me behind all alone.'

`I cannot take thee now, little one,' said Leonardo gently. `Thou art still too small, but later on thou shalt come to me and be my pupil. This I promise thee.'

It was but a weary wandering life that awaited Leonardo after he was forced to leave his home in Milan. It seemed as if it was his fate to begin many things but to finish nothing. For a while he lived in Rome, but he did little real work there.

For several years he lived in Florence and began to paint a huge battle–picture. There too he painted the famous portrait of Mona Lisa, which is now in Paris. Of all portraits that have ever been painted this is counted the most wonderful and perfect piece of work, although Leonardo himself called it unfinished.

By this time the master had fallen on evil days. All his pupils were gone, and his friends seemed to have forgotten him. He was sitting before the fire one stormy night, lonely and sad, when the door opened and a tall handsome lad came in.

`Master!' he cried, and kneeling down he kissed the old man's hands. `Dost thou not know me? I am thy little Francesco, come to claim thy promise that I should one day be thy servant and pupil.

Leonardo laid his hand upon the boy's fair head and looked into his face.

`I am growing old,' he said, `and I can no longer do for thee what I might once have done. I am but a poor wanderer now. Dost thou indeed wish to cast in thy lot with mine?'

`I care only to be near thee,' said the boy. `I will go with thee to the ends of the earth.'

So when, soon after, Leonardo received an invitation from the new King of France, he took the boy with him, and together they made their home in the little chateau of Claux near the town of Amboise.

The master's hair was silvered now, and his long beard was as white as snow. His keen blue eyes looked weary and tired of life, and care had drawn many deep lines on his beautiful face. Sad thoughts were always his company. The one word `failure' seemed to be written across his life. What had he done? He had begun many things and had finished but few. His great fresco was even now fading away and becoming dim and blurred. His model for the marvellous horse was destroyed. A few pictures remained, but these had never quite reached his ideal. The crowd who had once hailed him as the greatest of all artists, could now only talk of Michelangelo and the young Raphael. Michelangelo himself had once scornfully told him he was a failure and could finish nothing.

He was glad to leave Italy and all its memories behind, and he hoped to begin work again in his quiet little French home. But Death was drawing near, and before many years had passed he grew too weak to hold a brush or pencil.

It was in the springtime of the year that the end came. Francesco had opened the window and gently lifted the master in his strong young arms, that he might look once more on the outside world which he loved so dearly. The trees were putting on their dainty dress of tender green, white clouds swept across the blue sky, and April sunshine flooded the room.

As he looked out, the master's tired eyes woke into life.

`Look!' he cried, `the swallows have come back! Oh that they would lend me their wings that I might fly away and be at rest!'

The swallows darted and circled about in the clear spring air, busy with their building plans, but Francesco thought he heard the rustle of other wings, as the master's soul, freed from the tired body, was at last borne upwards higher than any earthly wings could soar.

RAPHAEL

Among the marvellous tales of the Arabian Nights, there is a story told of a band of robbers who, by whispering certain magic words, were able to open the door of a secret cave where treasures of gold and silver and precious jewels lay hid. Now, although the day of such delightful marvels is past and gone, yet there still remains a certain magic in some names which is able to open the secret doors of the hidden haunts of beauty and delight.

For most people the very name of `Raphael' is like the `Open Sesame' of the robber chief in the old story. In a moment a door seems to open out of the commonplace everyday world, and through it they see a stretch of fair sweet country. There their eyes rest upon gentle, dark–eyed Madonnas, who smile down lovingly upon the heavenly Child, playing at her side or resting in her arms. The little St. John is also there, companion of the Infant Christ; rosy, round–limbed children both, half human and half divine. And standing in the background are a crowd of grave, quiet figures, each one alive with interest, while over all there is a glow of intense vivid colour.

We know but little of the everyday life of this great artist. When we hear his name, it is of his different pictures that we think at once, for they are world–famous. We almost forget the man as we gaze at his work.

It was in the little village of Urbino, in Umbria, that Raphael was born. His father was a painter called Giovanni Santi, and from him Raphael inherited his love of Art. His mother, Magia, was a sweet, gracious woman, and the little Raphael was like her in character and beauty. It seemed as if the boy had received every good gift that Nature could bestow. He had a lovely oval face, and soft dark eyes that shone with a beauty that was more of heaven than earth, and told of a soul which was as pure and lovely as his face. Above all, he had the gift of making every one love him, so that his should have been a happy sunshiny life.

But no one can ever escape trouble, and when Raphael was only eight years old, the first cloud overspread his sky. His mother died, and soon after his father married again.

The new mother was very young, and did not care much for children, but Raphael did not mind that as long as he could be with his father. But three years later a blacker cloud arose and blotted out the sunshine from his life, for his father too died, and left him all alone.

The boy had loved his father dearly, and it had been his great delight to be with him in the studio, to learn to grind and mix the colours and watch those wonderful pictures grow from day to day.

But now all was changed. The quiet studio rang with angry voices, and the peaceful home was the scene of continual quarrelling. Who was to have the money, and how were the Santi estates to be divided? Stepmother and uncle wrangled from morning until night, and no one gave a thought to the child Raphael. It was only the money that mattered.

Then when it seemed that the boy's training was going to be totally neglected, kindly help arrived. Simone di Ciarla, brother of Raphael's own mother, came to look after his little nephew, and ere long carried him off from the noisy, quarrelsome household, and took him to Perugia.

`Thou shalt have the best teaching in all Italy,' said Simone as they walked through the streets of the town. `The great master to whose studio we go, can hold his own even among the artists of Florence. See that thou art diligent to learn all that he can teach thee, so that thou mayest become as great a painter as thy father.'

`Am I to be the pupil of the great Perugino?' asked Raphael, his eyes shining with pleasure. `I have often heard my father speak of his marvellous pictures.'

`We will see if he can take thee,' answered his uncle.

The boy's heart sunk. What if the master refused to take him as a pupil? Must he return to idleness and the place which was no longer home?

But soon his fears were set at rest. Perugino, like every one else, felt the charm of that beautiful face and gentle manner, and when he had seen some drawings which the boy had done, he agreed readily that Raphael should enter the studio and become his pupil.

Perugia had been passing through evil times just before this. The two great parties of the Oddi and Baglioni families were always at war together. Whichever of them happened to be the stronger held the city and drove out the other party, so that the fighting never ceased either inside or outside the gates. The peaceful country round about had been laid waste and desolate. The peasants did not dare go out to till their fields or prune their olive–trees. Mothers were afraid to let their little ones out of their sight, for hungry wolves and other wild beasts prowled about the deserted countryside.

Then came a day when the outside party managed to creep silently into the city, and the most terrible fight of all began. So long and fiercely did the battle rage that almost all the Oddi were killed. Then for a time there was peace in Perugia and all the country round.

So it happened that as soon as the people of Perugia had time to think of other things besides fighting, they began to wish that their town might be put in order, and that the buildings which had been injured during the struggles might be restored.

This was a good opportunity for peaceful men like Perugino, for there was much work to be done, and both he and his pupils were kept busy from morning till night.

Of all his pupils, Perugino loved the young Raphael best. He saw at once that this was no ordinary boy.

`He is my pupil now, but soon he will be my master,' he used to say as he watched the boy at work.

So he taught him with all possible carefulness, and was never tired of giving him good advice.

`Learn first of all to draw,' he would say, when Raphael looked with longing eyes at the colours and brushes of the master. `Draw everything you see, no matter what it is, but always draw and draw again. The rest will follow; but if the knowledge of drawing be lacking, nothing will afterwards succeed. Keep always at hand a sketch–book, and draw therein carefully every manner of thing that meets thy eye.'

Raphael never forgot the good advice of his master. He was never without a sketch–book, and his drawings now are almost as interesting as his great pictures, for they show the first thought that came into his mind, before the picture was composed.

So the years passed on, and Raphael learned all that the master could teach him. At first his pictures were so like Perugino's, that it was difficult to know whether they were the work of the master or the pupil.

But the quiet days at Perugia soon came to an end, and Perugino went back to Florence. For some time Raphael worked at different places near Perugia, and then followed his master to the City of Flowers, where every artist longed to go. Though he was still but a young man, the world had already begun to notice his work, and Florence gladly welcomed a new artist.

It was just at that time that Leonardo da Vinci's fame was at its height, and when Raphael was shown some of the great man's work, he was filled with awe and wonder. The genius of Leonardo held him spellbound.

`It is what I have dreamed of in my dreams,' he said. `Oh that I might learn his secret!'

Little by little the new ideas sunk into his heart, and the pictures he began to paint were no longer like those of his old master Perugino, but seemed to breathe some new spirit.

It was always so with Raphael. He seemed to be able to gather the best from every one, just as the bee goes from flower to flower and gathers its sweetness into one golden honeycomb. Only the genius of Raphael made all that he touched his very own, and the spirit of his pictures is unlike that of any other master.

For many years after this he lived in Rome, where now his greatest frescoes may be seen— frescoes so varied and wonderful that many books have been written about them.

There he first met Margarita, the young maiden whom he loved all his life. It is her face which looks down upon us from the picture of the Sistine Madonna, perhaps the most famous Madonna that ever was painted. The little room in the Dresden Gallery where this picture now hangs seems almost like a holy place, for surely there is something divine in that fair face. There she stands, the Queen of Heaven, holding in her arms the Infant Christ, with such a strange look of majesty and sadness in her eyes as makes us realise that she was indeed fit to be the Mother of our Lord.

80

But the picture which all children love best is one in Florence called `The Madonna of the Goldfinch.'

It is a picture of the Holy Family, the Infant Jesus, His mother, and the little St. John. The Christ Child is a dear little curly–headed baby, and He stands at His mother's knee with one little bare foot resting on hers. His hand is stretched out protectingly over a yellow goldfinch which St. John, a sturdy little figure clad in goatskins, has just brought to Him. The baby face is full of tender love and care for the little fluttering prisoner, and His curved hand is held over its head to protect it.

`Do not hurt My bird,' He seems to say to the eager St. John, `for it belongs to Me and to My Father.'

These are only two of the many pictures which Raphael painted. It is wonderful to think how much work he did in his short life, for he died when he was only thirty–seven. He had been at work at St. Peter's, giving directions about some alterations, and there he was seized by a severe chill, and in a few days the news spread like wildfire through the country that Raphael was dead.

It seemed almost as if it could not be true. He had been so full of life and health, so eager for work, such a living power among men.

But there he lay, beautiful in death as he had been in life, and over his head was hung the picture of the `Transfiguration,' on which he had been at work, its colours yet wet, never to be finished by that still hand.

All Rome flocked to his funeral, and high and low mourned his loss. But he left behind him a fame which can never die, a name which through all these four hundred years has never lost the magic of its greatness.

MICHELANGELO

Sometimes in a crowd of people one sees a tall man, who stands head and shoulders higher than any one else, and who can look far over the heads of ordinary– sized mortals.

`What a giant!' we exclaim, as we gaze up and see him towering above us.

So among the crowd of painters travelling along the road to Fame we see above the rest a giant, a greater and more powerful genius than any that came before or after him. When we hear the name of Michelangelo we picture to ourselves a great rugged, powerful giant, a veritable son of thunder, who, like the Titans of old, bent every force of Nature to his will.

This Michelangelo was born at Caprese among the mountains of Casentino. His father, Lodovico Buonarroti, was podesta or mayor of Caprese, and came of a very ancient and honourable family, which had often distinguished itself in the service of Florence.

Now the day on which the baby was born happened to be not only a Sunday, but also a morning when the stars were especially favourable. So the wise men declared that some heavenly virtue was sure to belong to a child born at that particular time, and without hesitation Lodovico determined to call his little son Michael Angelo, after the archangel Michael. Surely that was a name splendid enough to adorn any great career.

It happened just then that Lodovico's year of office ended, and so he returned with his wife and child to Florence. He had a property at Settignano, a little village just outside the city, and there he settled down.

Most of the people of the village were stone– cutters, and it was to the wife of one of these labourers that little Michelangelo was sent to be nursed. So in after years the great master often said that if his mind was worth anything, he owed it to the clear pure mountain air in which he was born, just as he owed his love of carving stone to the unconscious influence of his nurse, the stone– cutter's wife.

As the boy grew up he clearly showed in what direction his interest lay. At school he was something of a dunce at his lessons, but let him but have a pencil and paper and his mind was wide awake at once. Every spare moment he spent making sketches on the walls of his father's house.

But Lodovico would not hear of the boy becoming an artist. There were many children to provide for, and the family was not rich. It would be much more fitting that Michelangelo should go into the silk and woollen business and learn to make money.

But it was all in vain to try to make the boy see the wisdom of all this. Scold as they might, he cared for nothing but his pencil, and even after he was severely beaten he would creep back to his beloved work. How he envied his friend Francesco who worked in the shop of Master Ghirlandaio! It was a joy even to sit and listen to the tales of the studio, and it was a happy day when Francesco brought some of the master's drawings to show to his eager friend.

Little by little Lodovico began to see that there was nothing for it but to give way to the boy's wishes, and so at last, when he was fourteen years old, Michelangelo was sent to study as a pupil in the studio of Master Ghirlandaio.

It was just at the time when Ghirlandaio was painting the frescoes of the chapel in Santa Maria Novella, and Michelangelo learned many lessons as he watched the master at work, or even helped with the less important parts.

But it was like placing an eagle in a hawk's nest. The young eagle quickly learned to soar far higher than the hawk could do, and ere long began to `sweep the skies alone.'

It was not pleasant for the great Florentine master, whose work all men admired, to have his drawings corrected by a young lad, and perhaps Michelangelo was not as humble as he should have been. In the strength of his great knowledge he would sometimes say sharp and scornful things, and perhaps he forgot the respect due from pupil to master.

Be that as it may, he left Ghirlandaio's studio when he was sixteen years old, and never had another master. Thenceforward he worked out his own ideas in his giant strength, and was the pupil of none.

The boy Francesco was still his friend, and together they went to study in the gardens of San Marco, where Lorenzo the Magnificent had collected many statues and works of art. Here was a new field for Michelangelo. Without needing a lesson he began to copy the statues in terra–cotta, and so clever was his work that Lorenzo was delighted with it.

`See, now, what thou canst do with marble,' he said. `Terra–cotta is but poor stuff to work in.'

Michelangelo had never handled a chisel before, but he chipped and cut away the marble so marvellously that life seemed to spring out of the stone. There was a marble head of an old faun in the garden, and this Michelangelo set himself to copy. Such a wonderful copy did he make that Lorenzo was amazed. It was even better than the original, for the boy had introduced ideas of his own and had made the laughing mouth a little open to show the teeth and the tongue of the faun. Lorenzo noticed this, and turned with a smile to the young artist.

`Thou shouldst have remembered that old folks never keep all their teeth, but that some of them are always wanting,' he said.

Of course Lorenzo meant this as a joke, but Michelangelo immediately took his hammer and struck out several of the teeth, and this too pleased Lorenzo greatly.

There was nothing that the Magnificent ruler loved so much as genius, so Michelangelo was received into the palace and made the companion of Lorenzo's sons. Not only did good fortune thus smile upon the young artist, but to his great astonishment Lodovico too found that benefits were showered upon him, all for the sake of his famous young son.

These years of peace, and calm, steady work had the greatest effect on Michelangelo's work, and he learned much from the clever, brilliant men who thronged Lorenzo's court. Then, too, he first listened to that ringing voice which strove to raise Florence to a sense of her sins, when Savonarola preached his great sermons in the Duomo. That teaching sank deep into the heart of Michelangelo, and years afterwards he left on the walls of the Sistine Chapel a living echo of those thundering words.

Like all the other artists, he would often go to study Masaccio's frescoes in the little chapel of the Carmine. There was quite a band of young artists working there, and very soon they began to look with envious feelings at Michelangelo's drawings, and their jealousy grew as his fame increased. At last, one day, a youth called Torriggiano could bear it no longer, and began to make scornful remarks, and worked himself up into such a rage that he aimed a blow at Michelangelo with his fist, which not only broke his nose but crushed it in such a way that he was marked for life. He had had a rough, rugged look before this, but now the crooked nose gave him almost a savage expression which he never lost.

Changes followed fast after this time of quiet. Lorenzo the Magnificent died, and his son, the weak Piero de Medici, tried to take his place as ruler of Florence. For a time Michelangelo continued to live at the court of Piero, but it was not encouraging to work for a master whose foolish taste demanded statues to be made out of snow, which, of course, melted at the first breath of spring.

Michelangelo never forgot all that he owed to Lorenzo, and he loved the Medici family, but his sense of justice made him unable to take their part when trouble arose between them and the Florentine people. So when the struggle began he left Florence and went first to Venice and then to Bologna. From afar he heard how the weak Piero had been driven out of the city, but more bitter still was his grief when the news came that the solemn warning voice of the great preacher Savonarola was silenced for ever.

Then a great longing to see his beloved city again filled his heart, and he returned to Florence.

Botticelli was a sad, broken–down old man now, and Ghirlandaio was also growing old, but Florence was still rich in great artists. Leonardo da Vinci, Perugino, and Filippino Lippi were all there, and men talked of the coming of an even greater genius, the young Raphael of Urbino.

There happened just then to be at the works of the Cathedral of St. Mary of the Flowers a huge block of marble which no one knew how to use. Leonardo da Vinci had been invited to carve a statue out of it, but he had refused to try, saying he could do nothing with it. But when the marble was offered to Michelangelo his eye kindled and he stood for a long time silent before the great white block. Through the outer walls of stone he seemed to see the figure imprisoned in the marble, and his giant strength and giant mind longed to go to work to set that figure free.

And when the last covering of marble was chipped and cut away there stood out a magnificent figure of the young David. Perhaps he is too strong and powerful for our idea of the gentle shepherd–lad, but he is a wonderful figure, and Goliath might well have trembled to meet such a young giant.

People flocked to see the great statue, and many were the discussions as to where it should be placed. Artists were never tired of giving their opinion, and even of criticising the work. `It seems to me,' said one, `that the nose is surely much too large for the face. Could you not alter that?'

Michelangelo said nothing, but he mounted the scaffolding and pretended to chip away at the nose with his chisel. Meanwhile he let drop some marble chips and dust upon the head of the critic beneath. Then he came down.

`Is that better?' he asked gravely.

`Admirable!' answered the artist. `You have given it life.'

Michelangelo smiled to himself. How wise people thought themselves when they often knew nothing about what they were talking! But the critic was satisfied, and did not notice the smile.

It would fill a book to tell of all the work which Michelangelo did; but although he began so much, a great deal of it was left unfinished. If he had lived in quieter times, his work would have been more complete; but one after another his patrons died, or changed their minds, and set him to work at something else before he had finished what he was doing.

The great tomb which Pope Julius had ordered him to make was never finished, although Michelangelo drew out all the designs for it, and for forty years was constantly trying to complete it. The Pope began to think it was an evil omen to build his own tomb, so he made up his mind that Michelangelo should instead set to work to fresco the ceiling of the Sistine Chapel. In vain did the great sculptor repeat that he knew but little of the art of painting.

`Didst thou not learn to mix colours in the studio of Master Ghirlandaio?' said Julius. `Thou hast but to remember the lessons he taught thee. And, besides, I have heard of a great drawing of a battle– scene which thou didst make for the Florentines, and have seen many drawings of thine, one especially: a terrible head of a furious old man, shrieking in his rage, such as no other hand than thine could have drawn. Is there aught that thou canst not do if thou hast but the will?'

And the Pope was right; for as soon as Michelangelo really made up his mind to do the work, all difficulties seemed to vanish.

It was no easy task he had undertaken. To stand upright and cover vast walls with painting is difficult enough, but Michelangelo was obliged to lie flat upon a scaffolding and paint the ceiling above him. Even to look up at that ceiling for ten minutes makes the head and neck ache with pain, and we wonder how such a piece of work could ever have been done.

No help would the master accept, and he had no pupils. Alone he worked, and he could not bear to have any one near him looking on. In silence and solitude he lay there painting those marvellous frescoes of the story of the Creation to the time of Noah. Only Pope Julius himself dared to disturb the master, and he alone climbed the scaffolding and watched the work.

`When wilt thou have finished?' was his constant cry. `I long to show thy work to the world.'

`Patience, patience,' said Michelangelo. `Nothing is ready yet.'

`But when wilt thou make an end?' asked the impatient old man.

`When I can,' answered the painter.

Then the Pope lost his temper, for he was not accustomed to be answered like this.

`Dost thou want to be thrown head first from the scaffold?' he asked angrily. `I tell thee that will happen if the work is not finished at once.'

So, incomplete as they were, Michelangelo was obliged to uncover the frescoes that all Rome might see them. It was many years before the ceiling was finished or the final fresco of the Last Judgment painted upon the end wall.

Michelangelo lived to be a very old man, and his life was lonely and solitary to the end. The one woman he loved, Vittoria Colonna, had died, and with her death all brightness for him had faded. Although he worked so much in Rome, it was always Florence that he loved. There it was that he began the statues for the Chapel of the Medici, and there, too, he helped to build the defences of San Miniato when the Medici family made war upon the City of Flowers.

So when the great man died in Rome it seemed but fit that his body should be carried back to his beloved Florence. There it now rests in the Church of Santa Croce, while his giant works, his great and terrible thoughts breathed out into marble or flashed upon the walls of the Sistine Chapel, live on for ever, filling the minds of men with a great awe and wonder as they gaze upon them.

ANDREA DEL SARTO

Nowhere in Florence could a more honest man or a better worker be found than Agnolo the tailor. True, there were once evil tales whispered about him when he first opened his shop in the little street. It was said that he was no Italian, but a foreigner who had been obliged to flee from his own land because of a quarrel he had had with one of his customers. People shook their heads and talked mysteriously of how the tailor's scissors had been used as a deadly weapon in the fight. But ere long these stories died away, and the tailor, with his wife Constanza, lived a happy, busy life, and brought up their six children carefully and well.

Now out of those six children five were just the ordinary commonplace little ones such as one would expect to meet in a tailor's household, but the sixth was like the ugly duckling in the fairy tale—a little, strange bird, unlike all the rest, who learned to swim far away and soon left the old commonplace home behind him.

The boy's name was Andrea. He was such a quick, sharp little boy that he was sent very early to school, and had learned to read and write before he was seven years old. As that was considered quite enough education, his father then took him away from school and put him to work with a goldsmith.

It is early days to begin work at seven years old, but Andrea thought it was quite as good as play. He was always perfectly happy if he could have a pencil and paper, and his drawings and designs were really so wonderfully good that his master grew to be quite proud of the child and showed the work to all his customers.

Next door to the goldsmith's shop there lived an old artist called Barile, who began to take a great interest in little Andrea. Barile was not a great painter, but still there was much that he could teach the boy, and he was anxious to have him as a pupil. So it was arranged that Andrea should enter the studio and learn to be an artist instead of a goldsmith.

For three years the boy worked steadily with his new master, but by that time Barile saw that better teaching was needed than he could give. So after much thought the old man went to the great Florentine artist Piero di Cosimo, and asked him if he would agree to receive Andrea as his pupil. `You will find the boy no trouble,' he urged. `He has wonderful talent, and already he has learnt to mix his colours so marvellously that to my mind there is no artist in Florence who knows more about colour than little Andrea' Cosimo shook his head in unbelief. The boy was but a child, and this praise seemed absurd. However, the drawings were certainly extraordinary, and he was glad to receive so clever a pupil.

But little by little, as Cosimo watched the boy at work, his unbelief vanished and his wonder grew, until he was as fond and proud of his pupil as the old master had been. `He handles his colours as if he had had fifty years of experience,' he would say proudly, as he showed off the boy's work to some new patron.

And truly the knowledge of drawing and colouring seemed to come to the boy without any effort. Not that he was idle or trusted to chance. He was never tired of work, and his greatest joy on holidays was to go of and study the drawings of the great Michelangelo and Leonardo da Vinci. Often he would spend the whole day copying these drawings with the greatest care, never tired of learning more and more.

As Andrea grew older, all Florence began to take note of the young painter—`Andrea del Sarto,' as he was called, or `the tailor's Andrew,' for sarto is the Italian word for tailor.

What a splendid new star this was rising in the heaven of Art! Who could tell how bright it would shine ere long? Perhaps the tailor's son would yet eclipse the magic name of Raphael. His colour was perfect, his drawing absolutely correct. They called him in their admiration `the faultless painter.' But had he, indeed, the artist soul? That was the question. For, perfect as his pictures were, they still lacked something. Perhaps time would teach him to supply that want.

Meanwhile there was plenty of work for the young artist, and when he set up his own studio with another young painter, he was at once invited to fresco the walls of the cloister of the Scalzo, or bare– footed friars.

This was the happiest time of all Andrea's life. The two friends worked happily together, and spent many a merry day with their companions. Every day Andrea learned to add more softness and delicacy to his colouring until his pictures seemed verily to glow with life. Every day he dreamed fresh dreams of the fame and honour that awaited him. And when work was over, the two young painters would go off to meet their friends and make merry over their supper as they told all the latest jokes and wittiest stories, and forgot for a while the serious art of painting pictures.

There were twelve of these young men who met together, and each of them was bound to bring some particular dish for the general supper. Every one tried to think of something especially nice and uncommon, but no one managed such surprising delicacies as Andrea. There was one special dish which no one ever forgot. It was in the shape of a temple, with its pillars made of sausages. The pavement was formed of little squares of different coloured jelly, the tops of the pillars were cheese, and the roof was of sugar, with a frieze of sweets running round it. Inside the temple there was a choir of roast birds with their mouths wide open, and the priests were two fat pigeons. It was the most splendid supper–dish that ever was seen.

Every one was fond of the clever young painter. He was so kind and courteous to all, and so simple– hearted that it was impossible for the others to feel jealous or to grudge him the fame and praise that was showered upon him more and more as each fresh picture was finished.

Then just when all gave promise of sunshine and happiness, a little cloud rose in his blue sky, which grew and grew until it dimmed all the glory of his life.

In the Via di San Gallo, not very far from the street where Andrea and his friend lodged, there lived a very beautiful woman called Lucrezia. She was not a highborn lady, only the daughter of a working man, but she was as proud and haughty as she was beautiful. Nought cared she for things high and noble, she was only greedy of praise and filled with a desire to have her own way in everything. Yet her lovely face seemed as if it must be the mirror of a lovely soul, and when the young painter Andrea first saw her his heart went out towards her. She was his long–dreamed–of ideal of beauty and grace, the vision of loveliness which he had been trying to grasp all his life.

`What hath bewitched thee?' asked his friend as he watched Andrea restlessly pacing up and down the studio, his brushes thrown aside and his work left unfinished. `Thou hast done little work for many weeks.'

`I cannot paint,' answered Andrea, `for I see only one face ever before me, and it comes between me and my work.'

`Thou art ruining all thy chances,' said the friend sadly, `and the face thou seest is not worth the sacrifice.'

Andrea turned on his heel with an angry look and went out. All his friends were against him now. No one had a good word for the beautiful Lucrezia. But she was worth all the world to him, and he had made up his mind to marry her.

It was winter time, and the Christmas bells had but yesterday rung out the tidings of the Holy Birthday when Andrea at last obtained his heart's desire and made Lucrezia his wife. The joyful Christmastide seemed a fit season in which to set the seal upon his great happiness, and he thought himself the most fortunate of men. He had asked advice of none, and had told no one what he meant to do, but the news of his marriage was soon noised abroad.

`Hast thou heard the news of young Andrea del Sarto?' asked the people of Florence of one another. `I fear he has dealt an evil blow at his own chances of success.'

One by one his friends left him, and many of his pupils deserted the studio. Lucrezia's sharp tongue was unbearable, and she made mischief among them all. Only Andrea remained blinded by her beauty, and thought that now, with such a model always near him, he would paint as he had never painted before.

But little did Lucrezia care to help him with his work. His pictures meant nothing to her except so far as they sold well and brought in money for her to spend. Worst of all, she began to grudge the help that he gave to his old father and mother, who now were poor and needed his care.

And yet, although Andrea saw all this, he still loved his beautiful wife and cared only how he might please her. He scarcely painted a picture that had not her face in it, for she was his ideal Madonna, Queen of Heaven.

But it was not so easy now to put his whole heart and soul into his work. True, his hand drew as correctly as ever, and his colours were even more beautiful, but often the soul seemed lacking.

`Thou dost work but slowly,' the proud beauty would say, tired of sitting still as his model. `Why canst thou not paint quicker and sell at higher prices? I have need of more gold, and the money seems to grow scarcer week by week.'

Andrea sighed. Truly the money vanished like magic, as Lucrezia's jewels and dresses increased.

`Dear heart, have a little patience,' he said. `I can but do my best.'

Then, as he looked at the angry discontented face of his wife, he laid down his brushes and went to kneel beside her.

`Lucrezia,' he said, `there needs something besides mere drawing and painting to make a picture. They call me ``the faultless painter,'' and it seemed once as if I might have reached as high or even higher than the great Raphael. It needed but the soul put into my work, and if thou couldst have helped me to reach my ideal, what would I not have shown the world!'

`I do not understand thee,' said Lucrezia petulantly, `and this is waste of time. Haste thee and get back to thy brushes and paints, and see that thou drivest a better bargain with this last picture.'

No, it was no use; she could never understand! Andrea knew that he must look for no help from her, and that he must paint in spite of the hindrances she placed in his way. Well, his work was still considered most beautiful, and he must make the best of it.

Orders for pictures came now from far and near, and before long some of Andrea's work found its way into France; and when King Francis saw it he was so anxious to have the painter at his court, that he sent a royal invitation, begging Andrea to come at once to France and enter the king's service.

The invitation came when Andrea was feeling hopeless and dispirited. Lucrezia gave him no peace, the money was all spent, and he was weary of work. The thought of starting afresh in another country put new courage into him. He made up his mind to go at once to the French court. He would leave Lucrezia in some safe place and send her all the money he could earn.

How good it was to leave all his troubles behind, and to set off that glad May day when all the world breathed of new life and new hope. Perhaps the winter of his life was passed too, and only sunshine and summer was in store.

Andrea's welcome at the French court was most flattering. Nothing was thought too good for the famous Florentine painter, and he was treated like a prince. The king loaded him with gifts, and gave him costly clothes and money for all his needs. A portrait of the infant Dauphin was begun at once, for which Andrea received three hundred golden pieces.

Month after month passed happily by. Andrea painted many pictures, and each one was more admired than the last. But his dream of happiness did not last long. He was hard at work one day when a letter was brought to him, sent by his wife Lucrezia. She could not live without him, so she wrote. He must come home at once. If he delayed much longer he would not find her alive.

There could be, of course, but one answer to all this. Andrea loved his wife too well to think of refusing her request, and the days of peace and plenty must come to an end. Even as he read her letter he began to long to see her again, and the thought of showing her all his gay clothes and costly presents filled him with delight.

But the king was very loth to let the painter go, and only at last consented when Andrea promised most faithfully to return a few months hence.

`I cannot spare thee for longer,' said Francis; `but I will let thee go on condition that thou wilt buy for me certain works of art in Italy, which I have long coveted, and bring them back with thee.'

Then he entrusted to Andrea a large sum of money and bade him buy the best pictures he could find, and afterwards return without fail.

So Andrea journeyed back to Florence, and when he was once again with his wife, his joy and delight in her were so great that he forgot all his promises, forgot even the king's trust, and allowed Lucrezia to squander all the money which was to have been spent on art treasures for King Francis.

Then returned the evil days of trouble and quarrelling. Added to that the terrible feeling that he had betrayed his trust and broken his word, made Andrea more unhappy than ever. He dared not return to France, but took up again his work in Florence, always with the hope that he might make enough money to repay the debt.

Years went by and dark days fell upon the City of Flowers. She had made a great struggle for liberty and had driven out the Medici, but they were helped by enemies from without, and Florence was for many months in a state of siege. There was constant fighting going on and little time for peaceful work.

Yet through all those troubled days Andrea worked steadily at his painting, and paid but little heed to the fate of the city. The stir of battle did not reach his quiet studio. There was enough strife at home; no need to seek it outside.

It was about this time that he painted a beautiful picture for the Company of San Jacopo, which was used as a banner and carried in their processions. Bad weather, wind, rain, and sunshine have spoiled some of its beauty, but much of the loveliness still remains. It is specially a children's picture, for Andrea painted the great saint bending over a little child in a white robe who kneels at his feet, while another little figure kneels close by. The boy has his hands folded together as if in prayer, and the kind strong hand of the saint is placed lovingly beneath the little chin. The other child is holding a book, and both children press close against the robe of the protecting saint.

But although Andrea could paint his pictures undisturbed while war was raging around, there was one enemy waiting to enter Florence who claimed attention and could not be ignored. When the triumphant troops gained an entrance by treachery, they brought with them that deadly scourge which was worse than any earthly enemy, the dreadful illness called the plague.

Perhaps Andrea had suffered for want of good food during the siege, perhaps he was overworked and tired; but, whatever was the cause, he was one of the first to be seized by that terrible disease. Alone he fought the enemy, and alone he died. Lucrezia had left him as soon as he fell ill, for she feared the deadly plague, and Andrea gladly let her go, for he loved her to the last with the same great unselfish love.

So passed away the faultless painter, and his was the last great name engraved upon that golden record of Florentine Art which had made Florence famous in the eyes of the world. Other artists came after him, but Art was on the wane in the City of Flowers, and her glory was slowly departing.

We can trace no other great name upon her pages and so we close the book, and our eyes turn towards the shores of the blue Adriatic, where Venice, Queen of the Sea, was writing, year by year, another volume filled with the names of her own Knights of Art.

GIOVANNI BELLINI

Almost all the stories of the lives of the painters which we have been listening to, until now, have clustered round Florence, the City of Flowers. She was their great mother, and her sons loved her with a deep, passionate love, thinking nothing too fair with which to deck her beauty. Wherever they wandered she drew them back, for their very heartstrings were wound around her, and each and all strove to give her of their best.

But now we come to the stories of men whose lives gather round a different centre. Instead of the great mother–city beside the Arno, with her strong towers and warlike citizens, the noise of battle ever sounding in her streets, and her flowery fields encircling her on every side, we have now Venice, Queen of the Sea.

No warlike tread or tramp of angry crowds disturbs her fair streets, for here are no pavements, only the cool green water which laps the walls of her marble palaces, and gives back the sound of the dipping oar and the soft echo of passing voices, as the gondolas glide along her watery ways. Here are no grim grey towers of defence, but fairy palaces of white and coloured marbles, which rise from the waters below as if they had been built by the sea nymphs, who had fashioned them of their own sea– shells and mother–of–pearl.

There are no flowery meadows here, but instead the vast waters of the lagoons, which reach out until they meet the blue arc of the sky or touch the distant mountains which lie like a purple line upon the horizon. Here and there tiny islands lie upon its bosom, so faint and fairylike that they scarcely seem like solid land, reflected as they are in the transparent water.

But although Venice has no meadows decked with flowers and no wealth of blossoming trees, everywhere on every side she shines with colour, this wonderful sea–girt city. Her white marble palaces glow with a soft amber light, the cool green water that reflects her beauty glitters in rings of gold and blue, changing from colour to colour as each ripple changes its form. At sunset, when the sun disappears over the edge of the lagoon and leaves behind its trail of shining clouds, she is like a dream–city rising from a sea of molten gold—a double city, for in the pure gold is reflected each tower and spire, each palace and campanile, in masses of pale yellow and quivering white light, with here and there a burning touch of flame colour. She seems to have no connection with the solid, ordinary cities of the world. There she lies in all her beauty, silent and apart, like a white sea–bird floating upon the bosom of the ocean.

Venice had always seemed separate and distinct from the rest of the world. Her cathedral of San Marco was never under the rule of Rome, and her rulers, or doges, as they were called, governed the city as kings, and did not trouble themselves with the affairs of other towns. Her merchant princes sailed to far countries and brought home precious spoils to add to her beauty. Everything was as rich and rare and splendid as it was possible to make it, and she was unlike any other city on earth.

So the painters who lived and worked in this city of the sea had their own special way of painting, which was different to that of the Florentine school.

From their babyhood these men had looked upon all this beauty of colour, and the love of it had grown with their growth. The golden light on the water, the pearly–grey and tinted marbles, the gay sails of the galleys which swept the lagoons like painted butterflies, the wide stretch of water ending in the mystery of the distant skyline—it all sank into their hearts, and it was little wonder that they should strive to paint colour above all things, and at last reach a perfection such as no other school of painters has equalled.

As with the Florentine artists, so with these Venetian painters, we must leave many names unnoticed just now, and learn first to know those which shine out clearest among the many bright stars of fame.

In the beginning of the fifteenth century, four hundred years ago, when Fra Filippo Lippi was painting in Florence, there lived in Venice a certain Jacopo Bellini, who was a painter, and who had two sons called Gentile and Giovanni. The father taught his boys with great care, and gave them the best training he could, for he was anxious that his sons should become great painters. He saw that they were both clever and quick to learn, and he hoped great things of them.

`Never do less than your very best,' he would say, as he taught the boys how to draw and use their colours. `See how the Tuscan artists strive with one another, each desiring to do most honour to their city of Florence. So, Gentile, I would have thee also strive to be great; and thou, Giovanni, endeavour to be even greater than thy brother.'

But though the boys were thus taught to try and outdo each other, still they were always the best of friends, and there was never any unkind rivalry between them.

Gentile, the eldest, was fond of painting story pictures, which told the history of Venice, and showed the magnificent doges, and nobles, and people of the city, dressed in their rich robes. The Venetians loved pictures which showed forth the glory of their city, and very soon Gentile was invited to paint the walls of the Ducal Palace with his historical pictures.

Now Venice carried on a great trade with her ships, which sailed to many foreign lands. These ships, loaded with merchandise, touched at different ports, and the merchants sold their goods or took in exchange other things which they brought back to Venice. It happened that one of the ships which set sail for Turkey had on board among other things several pictures painted by Giovanni Bellini. These were shown to the Sultan of Turkey, who had never seen a picture before, and he was amazed and delighted beyond words. His religion forbade the making of pictures, but he paid no attention now to that law, but sent a messenger to Venice praying that the painter Bellini might come to him at once.

The rulers of Venice were unwilling to spare Giovanni just then, but they allowed Gentile to go, as his work at the Ducal Palace was finished.

So Gentile took his canvases and paints, and, setting sail in one of the merchant ships, soon arrived at the court of the Grand Turk.

He was received with every honour, and nothing was thought too good for this wonderful painter, who could make pictures which looked like living men. The Sultan loaded him with gifts and favours, and he lived there like a royal prince. Each picture painted by Gentile was thought more wonderful than the last. He painted a portrait of the Sultan, and even one of himself, which was considered little short of magic.

Thus a whole year passed by, and Gentile had a most delightful time and was well contented, until one day something happened which disturbed his peace.

He had painted a picture of the dancing daughter of Herodias, with the head of John the Baptist in her hand, and when it was finished he brought it and presented it to the Sultan.

As usual, the Sultan was charmed with the new picture; but he paused in his praises of its beauty, and looked thoughtfully at the head of St. John, and then frowned.

`It seems to me,' he said, `that there is something not quite right about that head. I do not think a head which had just been cut off would look exactly as that does in your picture.'

Gentile answered courteously that he did not wish to contradict his royal highness, but it seemed to him that the head was right.

`We shall see,' said the Sultan calmly, and he turned carelessly to a guard who stood close by and bade him cut of the head of one of the slaves, that Bellini might see if his picture was really correctly painted.

This was more than Gentile could stand.

`Who knows,' he said to himself, `that the Sultan may not wish to see next how my head would look cut off from my body!'

So while his precious head was still safe upon his shoulders he thought it wiser to slip quietly away and return to Venice by the very first ship he could find.

Meanwhile Giovanni had worked steadily on, and had far surpassed both his father and his brother. Indeed, he had become the greatest painter in Venice, the first of that wonderful Venetian school which learned to paint such marvellous colour.

With all the wealth of delicate shading spread out before his eyes, with the ever–changing wonder of the opal–tinted sea meeting him on every side, it was not strange that the love of colour sank into his very heart. In his pictures we can see the golden glow which bathes the marble palaces, the clear green of the water, the pure blues and burning crimsons all as transparent as crystal, not mere paint but living colour.

Giovanni did not care to paint stories of Venice, with great crowds of figures, as Gentile did. He loved best the Madonna and saints, single figures full of quiet dignity. His saints are more human than those which Fra Angelico painted, and yet they are not mere men and women, but something higher and nobler. Instead of the angels swinging their censers which the painter of San Marco so lovingly drew, Giovanni's angels are little human boys, with grave sweet faces; happy children with a look of heaven in their eyes, as they play on their little lutes and mandolines.

But besides the pictures of saints and angels, Giovanni had a wonderful gift for painting portraits, and most of the great people of Venice came to be painted by him. In our own National Gallery we have the portrait of the Doge Loredan, which is one of those pictures which can teach you many things when you have learned to look with seeing eyes.

So the brothers worked together, but before long death carried off the elder, and Giovanni was left alone.

Though he was now very old, Giovanni worked harder than ever, and his hand, instead of losing power, seemed to grow stronger and more and more skilful. He was ninety years old when he died, and he worked almost up to the last.

The brothers were both buried in the church of SS. Giovanni e Paolo, in the heart of Venice. There, in the dim quietness of the old church, they lie at rest together, undisturbed by the voices of the passers–by in the square outside, or the lapping of the water against the steps, as the tides ebb and flow around their quiet resting–place.

VITTORE CARPACCIO

Knights of the Art: Stories

Like most of the other great painters, Giovanni Bellini had many pupils working under him—boys who helped their master, and learned their lessons by watching him work. Among these pupils was a boy called Vittore Carpaccio, a sharp, clever lad, with keen bright eyes which noticed everything. No one else learned so quickly or copied the master's work so faithfully, and when in time he became himself a famous painter, his work showed to the end traces of the master's influence.

He must have been a curious boy, this Vittore Carpaccio, for although we know but little of his life, his pictures tell us many a tale about him.

In the olden days, when Venice was at the height of her glory, splendid fetes were given in the city, and the gorgeous shows were a wonder to behold. Early in the morning of these festa days, Carpaccio would steal away in the dim light from the studio, before the others were astir. Work was left behind, for who could work indoors on days like these? There was a holiday feeling in the very air. Songs and laughter and the echo of merry voices were heard on every side, and the city seemed one vast playground, where all the grown-up children as well as the babies were ready to spend a happy holiday.

The little side-streets of Venice, cut up by canals, seem like a veritable maze to those who do not know the city, but Carpaccio could quickly thread his way from bridge to bridge, and by many a short cut arrive at last at the great central water street of Venice, the Grand Canal. Here it was easy to find a corner from which he could see the gay pageant, and enjoy as good a view as any of those great people who would presently come out upon the balconies of their marble palaces.

The bridge of the Rialto, which throws its white span across the centre of the canal, was Carpaccio's favourite perch, for from here he could see the markets and the long row of marble palaces on either side. From every window hung gay-coloured tapestry, Turkey carpets, silken draperies, and delicate-tinted stuffs covered with Eastern embroideries. The market was crowded with a throng of holiday-makers, a garden of bright colours and from the balconies above richly dressed ladies looked down, themselves a pageant of beauty, with their wonderful golden hair and gleaming jewels, while green and crimson parrots, fastened by golden chains to the marble balustrades, screamed and flapped their wings, and delighted Carpaccio's keen eyes with their vivid beauty.

Then the procession of boats swept up the great waterway, and the blaze of colour made the boy hold his breath in sheer delight. The painted galleys, the rowers in their quaint dresses–half one colour and half another—with jaunty feathered caps upon their floating curls, the nobles and rulers in their crimson robes, the silken curtains of every hue trailing their golden fringes in the cool green water, as the boats glided past, all made up a picture which the boy never forgot.

Then when it was all over, Carpaccio would climb down and make his way back to the master's studio, and with the gay scene ever before his eyes would try, day after day, to paint every detail just as he had seen it.

There is another thing which we learn about Carpaccio from his pictures, and that is, that he must have loved to listen to old legends and stories of the saints, and that he stored them up in his mind, just as he treasured the remembrance of the gay processions and the flapping wings of those crimson and green parrots.

So, when he grew to be a man, and his fame began to spread, the first great pictures he painted were of the story of St. Ursula, told in loving detail, as only one who loved the story could do it.

But though Carpaccio might paint pictures of these old stories, it was always through the golden haze of Venice that he saw them. His St. Ursula is a dainty Venetian lady, and the bedroom in which she dreams her wonderful dream is just a room in one of the old marble palaces, with a pot of pinks upon the window–sill, and her little high–heeled Venetian shoes by the bedside. Whenever it was possible, Carpaccio would paint in those scenes on which his eyes had rested since his childhood—the painted galleys with their sails reflected in the clear water, the dainty dresses of the Venetian ladies, their gay–coloured parrots, pet dogs, and grinning monkeys.

In an old church of Venice there are some pictures said to have been painted by Carpaccio when he was a little boy only eight years old. They are scenes taken from the Bible stories, and very funny scenes they are too. But they show already what clever little hands and what a thinking head the boy had, and how Venice was the background in his mind for every story. For here is the meeting of the Queen of Sheba and King Solomon, and instead of Jerusalem with all its glory, we see a little wooden bridge, with King Solomon on one side and the Queen of Sheba on the other, walking towards each other, as if they were both in Venice crossing one of the little canals.

There were many foreign sailors in Venice in those old days, who came in the trading–ships from distant lands. Many of them were poor and unable to earn money to buy food, and when they were ill there was no one to look after them or help them. So some of the richer foreigners founded a Brotherhood, where the poor sailors might be helped in time of need. This Brotherhood chose St. George as their patron saint, and when they had built a little chapel they invited Carpaccio to come and paint the walls with pictures from the life of St. George and other saints.

Nothing could have suited Carpaccio better, and he began his work with great delight, for he had still his child's love of stories, and he would make them as gay and wonderful as possible. There we see St. George thundering along on his war–horse, with flying hair, clad in beautiful armour, the most perfect picture of a chivalrous knight. Then comes the dragon breathing out flames and smoke, the most awesome dragon that ever was seen; and there too is the picture of St. Tryphonius taming the terrible basilisk. The little boy–saint has folded his hands together, and looks upward in prayer, paying little heed to the evil glare of the basilisk, who prances at his feet. A crowd of gaily dressed courtiers stand whispering and watching behind the marble steps, and here again in the background we have the canals and bridges of Venice, the marble palaces and gay carpets hung from out the windows. Everything is of the very best of its kind, and painted with the greatest care, even to the design of the inlaid work on the marble steps.

As we pass from picture to picture, we wish we had known this Carpaccio, for he must have been a splendid teller of stories; and how he would have made us shiver with his dragons and his basilisks, and laugh over the antics of his little boys and girls, his scarlet parrots and green lizards.

But although we cannot hear him tell his stories, he still speaks through those wonderful old pictures which you will some day see when you visit the fairyland of Italy, and pay your court to Venice, Queen of the Sea

GIORGIONE

As we look back upon the lives of the great painters we can see how each one added some new knowledge to the history of Art, and unfolded fresh beauties to the eyes of the world. Very gradually all this was done, as a bud slowly unfolds its petals until the full-blown flower shows forth its perfect beauty. But here and there among the painters we find a man who stands apart from the rest, one who takes a new and almost startling way of his own. He does not gradually add new truths to the old ones, but makes an entirely new scheme of his own. Such a man was Giorgione, whose story we tell to-day.

It was at the same time as Leonardo da Vinci was the talk of the Florentine world, that another great genius was at work in Venice, setting his mark high above all who had gone before. Giorgio Barbarelli was born at Castel Franco, a small town not far from Venice, and it was to the great city of the sea that he was sent as soon as he was old enough, there to be trained under the famous Bellini. He was a handsome boy, tall and well-built, and with such a royal bearing that his companions at once gave him the name of Giorgione, or George the Great. And, as so often happened in those days, the nick- name clung to him, so that while his family name is almost forgotten he is still known as Giorgione.

There was much of the poet nature about Giorgione, and his love of music was intense. He composed his own songs and sang them to his own music upon the lute, and indeed it seemed as if there were few things which this Great George could not do. But it was his painting that was most wonderful, for his painted men and women seemed alive and real, and he caught the very spirit of music in his pictures and there held it fast.

Giorgione early became known as a great artist, and when he was quite a young man he was employed by the city of Venice to fresco the outside walls of the new German Exchange. Wind and rain and the salt sea air have entirely ruined these frescoes now, and there are but few of Giorgione's pictures left to us, but that perhaps makes them all the more precious in our eyes.

Even his drawings are rare, and the one you see here is taken from a bigger sketch in the Uffizi Gallery of Florence. It shows a man in Venetian dress helping two women to mount one of the niches of a marble palace in order to see some passing show, and to be out of the way of the crowd.

There is a picture now in the Venice Academy said to have been painted by Giorgione, which would interest every boy and girl who loves old stories. It tells the tale of an old Venetian legend, almost forgotten now, but which used to be told with bated breath, and was believed to be a matter of history. The story is this:

On the 25th of February 1340 a terrible storm began to rage around Venice, more terrible than any that had ever been felt before. For three days the wild winds swept her waters and shrieked around her palaces, churning up the sea into great waves and shaking the city to her very foundations. Lightning and thunder never ceased, and the rain poured down in a great sheet of grey water, until it seemed as if a second flood had come to visit the world. Slowly but surely the waters rose higher and higher, and Venice sunk lower and lower, and men said that unless the storm soon ceased the city would be overwhelmed. No one ventured out on the canals, and only an old fisherman who happened to be in his boat was swept along by the canal of San Marco, and managed with great difficulty to reach the steps. Very thankful to be safe on land he tied his boat securely, and sat down to wait until the storm should cease. As he sat there watching the lightning and hearing nothing but the shriek of the tempest, some one touched his shoulder and a stranger's voice sounded in his ear.

`Good fisherman,' it said, `wilt thou row me over to San Giorgio Maggiore? I will pay thee well if thou wilt go.'

The fisherman looked across the swirling waters to where the tall bell–tower upon the distant island could just be seen through the driving mist and rain.

`How is it possible to row across to San Giorgio?' he asked. `My little boat could not live for five minutes in those raging waters.'

But the stranger only insisted the more, and besought him to do his best.

So, as the fisherman was a hardy old man and had a bold, brave soul, he loosed the boat and set off in all the storm. But, strangely enough, it was not half so bad as he had feared, and before long the little boat was moored safely by the steps of San Giorgio Maggiore.

Here the stranger left the boat, but bade the fisherman wait his return.

Presently he came back, and with him came a young man, tall and strong, bearing himself with a knightly grace.

`Row now to San Niccolo da Lido,' commanded the stranger.

`How can I do that?' asked the fisherman in great fear. For San Niccolo was far distant, and he was rowing with but one oar, which is the custom in Venice.

`Row boldly, for it shall be possible for thee, and thou shalt be well paid,' replied the stranger calmly.

So, seeing it was the will of God, the fisherman set out once more, and, as they went, the waters spread themselves out smoothly before them, until they reached the distant San Niccolo da Lido.

Here an old man with a white beard was awaiting them, and when he too had entered the boat, the fisherman was commanded to row out towards the open sea.

Now the tempest was raging more fiercely than ever, and lo! across the wild waste of foaming waters an enormous black galley came bearing down upon them. So fast did it approach that it seemed almost to fly upon the wings of the wind, and as it came near the fisherman saw that it was manned by fearful–looking black demons, and knew that they were on their way to overwhelm the fair city of Venice.

But as the galley came near the little boat, the three men stood upright, and with outstretched arms made high above them the sign of the cross, and commanded the demons to depart to the place from whence they had come.

In an instant the sea became calm, and with a horrible shriek the demons in their black galley disappeared from view.

Then the three men ordered the fisherman to return as he had come. So the old man was landed at San Niccolo da Lido, the young knight at San Giorgio Maggiore, and, last of all, the stranger landed at San Marco.

Now when the fisherman found that his work was done, he thought it was time that he should receive his payment. For, although he had seen the great miracle, he had no mind to forgo his proper fare.

`Thou art right,' said the stranger, when the fisherman made his demand, `and thou shalt indeed be well paid. Go now to the Doge and tell him all thou hast seen; how Venice would have been destroyed by the demons of the tempest, had it not been for me and my two companions. I am St. Mark, the protector of your city; the brave young knight is St. George, and the old man whom we took in last is St. Nicholas. Tell the Doge that I bade him pay thee well for thy brave service.'

`But, and if I tell them this story, how will they believe that I speak the truth?' asked the fisherman.

Then St. Mark took a ring off his finger, and placed it in the fisherman's rough palm. `Thou shalt show them this ring as a proof,' he said; `and when they look in the treasury of San Marco, they will find that it is missing from there.'

And when he had finished saying this, St. Mark disappeared.

Then the next day, as early as possible, the fisherman went to the Doge and told his marvellous tale and showed the saint's ring. At first no one could believe the wild story, but when they sent and searched in St. Mark's treasury, lo! the ring was missing. Then they knew that it must indeed have been St. Mark who had appeared to the old fisherman, and had saved their beloved city from destruction.

So a solemn thanksgiving service was sung in the great church of San Marco, and the fisherman received his due reward.

He was no longer obliged to work for his living, but received a pension from the rulers of the city, so that he lived in comfort all the rest of his days.

In the picture we see the great black galley manned by the demons, sweeping down upon the little boat, in which the three saints stand upright. And not only are the demons on board their ship, but some are riding on dolphins and curious−looking fish, and the little boat is entirely surrounded by the terrible crew.

We do not know much about Giorgione's life, but we do know that it was a short and sad one, clouded over at the end by bitter sorrow. He had loved a beautiful Venetian girl, and was just about to marry her when a friend, whom he also loved, carried her off and left him robbed of love and friendship. Nothing could comfort him for his loss, the light seemed to have faded from his life, and soon life itself began to wane. A very little while after and he closed his eyes upon all the beauty and promise which had once filled his world. But though we have so few of his pictures, those few alone are enough to show that it was more than an idle jest which made his companions give him the nickname of George the Great.

TITIAN

We have seen how most of the great painters loved to paint into their pictures those scenes which they had known when they were boys, and which to the end of their lives they remembered clearly and vividly. A Giotto never forgets the look of his sheep on the bare hillside of Vespignano, Fra Angelico paints his heavenly pictures with the colours of spring flowers found on the slopes of Fiesole, Perugino delights in the wide spaciousness of the Umbrian plains with the winding river and solitary cypresses.

So when we come to the great Venetian painter Titian we look first with interest to see in what manner of a country he was born, and what were the pictures which Nature mirrored in his mind when he was still a boy.'

At the foot of the Alps, three days' journey from Venice, lies the little town of Cadore on the Pieve, and here it was that Titian was born. On every side rise great masses of rugged mountains towering up to the sky, with jagged peaks and curious fantastic shapes. Clouds float around their summits, and the mist will often wrap them in gloom and give them a strange and awesome look. At the foot of the craggy pass the mountain–torrent of the Pieve roars and tumbles on its way. Far–reaching forests of trees, with weather–beaten gnarled old trunks, stand firm against the mountain storms. Beneath their wide–spreading boughs there is a gloom almost of twilight, showing peeps here and there of deep purple distances beyond.

Small wonder it was that Titian should love to paint mountains, and that he should be the first to paint a purely landscape picture. He lived those strange solemn mountains and the wild country round, the deep gloom of the woods and the purple of the distance beyond.

The boy's father, Gregorio Vecelli, was one of the nobles of Cadore, but the family was not rich, and when Titian was ten years old he was sent to an uncle in Venice to be taught some trade. He had always been fond of painting, and it is said that when he was a very little boy he was found trying to paint a picture with the juices of flowers. His uncle, seeing that the boy had some talent, placed him in the studio of Giovanni Bellini.

But though Titian learned much from Bellini, it was not until he first saw Giorgione's work that he dreamed of what it was possible to do with colour. Thenceforward he began to paint with that marvellous richness of colouring which has made his name famous all over the world.

At first young Titian worked with Giorgione, and together they began to fresco the walls of the Exchange above the Rialto bridge. But by and by Giorgione grew jealous. Titian's work was praised too highly; it was even thought to be the better of the two. So they parted company, for Giorgione would work with him no more.

Venice soon began to awake to the fact that in Titian she had another great painter who was likely to bring fame and honour to the fair city. He was invited to finish the frescoes in the Grand Council–chamber which Bellini had begun, and to paint the portraits of the Doges, her rulers.

These portraits which Titian painted were so much admired that all the great princes and nobles desired to have themselves painted by the Venetian artist. The Emperor Charles V. himself when he stopped at Bologna sent to Venice to fetch Titian, and so delighted was he with his work that he made the painter a knight with a pension of two hundred crowns.

Fame and wealth awaited Titian wherever he went, and before long he was invited to Rome that he might paint the portrait of the Pope. There it was that he met Michelangelo, and that great master looked with much interest at the work of the Venetian artist and praised it highly, for the colouring was such as he had never seen equalled before

`It is most beautiful,' he said afterwards to a friend; `but it is a pity that in Venice they do not teach men how to draw as well as how to colour. If this Titian drew as well as he painted, it would be impossible to surpass him.'

But ordinary eyes can find little fault with Titian's drawing, and his portraits are thought to be the most wonderful that ever were painted. The golden glow of Venice is cast like a magic spell over his pictures, and in him the great Venetian school of colouring reaches its height.

Besides painting portraits, Titian painted many other pictures which are among the world's masterpieces.

He must have had a special love for children, this famous old Venetian painter. We can tell by his pictures how well he understood them and how he loved to paint them. He would learn much by watching his own little daughter Lavinia as she played about the old house in Venice. His wife had died, and his eldest son was only a grief and disappointment to his father, but the little daughter was the light of his eyes.

We seem to catch a glimpse of her face in his famous picture of the little Virgin going up the steps to the temple. The little maid is all alone, for she has left her companions behind, and the crowd stands watching her from below, while the high priest waits for her above. One hand is stretched out, and with the other she lifts her dress as she climbs up the marble steps. She looks a very real child with her long plait of golden hair and serious little face, and we cannot help thinking that the painter's own little daughter must have been in his mind when he painted the little Virgin.

Titian lived to be a very old man, almost a hundred years old, and up to the last he was always seen with the brush in his hand, painting some new picture. So, when he passed away, he left behind a rich store of beauty, which not only decked the walls of his beloved Venice, but made the whole world richer and more beautiful.

TINTORETTO

It was between four and five hundred years ago that Venice sat most proudly on her throne as Queen of the Sea. She had the greatest fleet in all the Mediterranean. She bought and sold more than any other nation. She had withstood the shock of battle and conquered all her foes, and now she had time to deck herself with all the beauty which art and wealth could produce.

The merchants of Venice sailed to every port and carried with them wonderful shiploads of goods, for which their city was famous—silks, velvets, lace, and rich brocades. The secret of the marvellous Tyrian dyes had been discovered by her people, and there were many dyers in Venice who were specially famous for the purple dye of Tyre, which was thought to be the most beautiful in all the world. Then too they had learned the art of blowing glass into fairy–like forms, as delicate and light as a bubble, catching in it every shade of colour, and twisting it into a hundred exquisite shapes. Truly there had never been a richer or more beautiful city than this Queen of the Sea.

It was just when the glory of Venice was at its highest that Art too reached its height, and Giorgione and Titian began to paint the walls of her palaces and the altarpieces of her churches.

In the very centre of the city where the poorer Venetians had their houses, there lived about this time a man called Battista Robusti who was a dyer, or `tintore,' as he is called in Italy. It was his little son Jacopo who afterwards became such a famous artist. His grand–sounding name `Tintoretto' means nothing but `the little dyer,' and it was given to him because of his father's trade.

Tintoretto must have been brought up in the midst of gorgeous colours. Not only did he see the wonderful changing tints of the outside world, but in his father's workshop he must often have watched the rich Venetian stuffs lifted from the dye vats, heavy with the crimson and purple shades for which Venice was famous. Perhaps all this glowing colour wearied his young eyes, for when he grew to be a man his pictures show that he loved solemn and dark tones, though he could also paint the most brilliant colours when he chose.

Of course, the boy Tintoretto began by painting the walls of his father's house, as soon as he was old enough to learn the use of dyes and paints. Even if he had not had in him the artist soul, he could scarcely have resisted the temptation to spread those lovely colours on the smooth white walls. Any child would have done the same, but Tintoretto's mischievous fingers already showed signs of talent, and his father, instead of scolding him for wasting colours and spoiling the walls, encouraged him to go on with his pictures.

As the boy grew older, his great delight was to wander about the city and watch the men at work building new palaces. But especially did he linger near those walls which Titian and Giorgione were covering with their wonderful frescoes. High on the scaffolding he would see the painters at work, and as he watched the boy would build castles in the air, and dream dreams of a time when he too would be a master–painter, and be bidden by Venice to decorate her walls.

To Tintoretto's mind Titian was the greatest man in all the world, and to be taught by him the greatest honour that heart could wish. So it was perhaps the happiest day in all his life when his father decided to take him to Titian's studio and ask the master to receive him as a pupil.

But the happiness lasted but a very short time. Titian did not approve of the boy's work, and refused to keep him in the studio; so poor, disappointed Tintoretto went home again, and felt as if all sunshine and hope had gone for ever from his life. It was a bitter disappointment to his father and mother too, for they had set their hearts on the boy becoming an artist. But in spite of all this, Tintoretto did not lose heart or give up his dreams. He worked on by himself in his own way, and Titian's paintings taught him many things even though the master himself refused to help him. Then too he saw some work of the great Michelangelo, and learned many a lesson from that. Thenceforward his highest ideal was always `the drawing of Michelangelo and the colour of Titian.

The young artist lived in a poor, bare room, and most of his money went in the buying of little pieces of old sculpture or casts. He had a very curious way of working the designs for his pictures. Instead of drawing many sketches, he made little wax models of figures and arranged them inside a cardboard or wooden box in which there was a hole to admit a lighted candle. So, besides the grouping of the figures, he could also arrange the light and shade.

But, though he worked hard, fame was long in coming to Tintoretto. People did not understand his way of painting. It was not after the manner of any of the great artists, and they were rather afraid of his bold, furious–looking work.

Nevertheless Tintoretto worked steadily on, always hoping, and whenever there was a chance of doing any work, even without receiving payment for it, he seized it eagerly.

It happened just then that the young Venetian artists had agreed to have a show of their paintings, and had hired a room for the exhibition in the Merceria, the busiest part of Venice.

Tintoretto was very glad of the chance of showing his work, so he sent in a portrait of himself and also one of his brother. As soon as these pictures were seen people began to take more notice of the clever young painter, and even Titian allowed that his work was good. His portraits were always fresh and life– like, and he drew with a bold strong touch, as you will see if you look at the drawing I have shown you —the head of a Venetian boy, such as Tintoretto met daily among the fisher–folk of Venice.

From that time Fortune began to smile on Tintoretto. Little by little work began to come in. He was asked to paint altarpieces for the churches, and even at last, when his name became famous, he was invited to work upon the walls of the Ducal Palace, the highest honour which a Venetian painter could hope to win.

The days of the poor, bare studio, and lonely, sad life were ended now. Tintoretto had no longer to struggle with poverty and neglect. His house was a beautiful palace looking over the lagoon towards Murano, and he had married the daughter of a Venetian noble, and lived a happy, contented life. Children's voices made gay music in his home, and the pattering of little feet broke the silence of his studio. Fame had come to him too. His work might be strange but it was very wonderful, and Venice was proud of her new painter. His great stormy pictures had earned for him the name off `the furious painter,' and the world began to acknowledge his greatness.

But the real sunshine of his life was his little daughter Marietta. As soon as she learned to walk she found her way to her father's studio, and until she was fifteen years old she was always with him and helped him as if she had been one of his pupils. She was dressed too as a boy, and visitors to the studio never guessed that the clever, handsome boy was really the painter's daughter.

There were many great schools in Venice at that time, and there was much work to be done in decorating their walls with paintings. A school was not really a place of education, but a society of people who joined themselves together in charity to nurse the sick, bury the dead, and release any prisoners who had been taken captive. One of the greatest of the schools was the `Scuola de San Rocco,' and this was given into the hands of Tintoretto, who covered the walls with his paintings, leaving but little room for other artists.

But it is in the Ducal Palace that the master's most famous work is seen. There, covering the entire side of the great hall, hangs his `Paradiso,' the largest oil painting in the world.

At first it seems but a gloomy picture of Paradise. It is so vast, and such hundreds of figures are crowded together, and the colour is dark and sombre. There is none of that swinging of golden censers by white– robed angels, none of the pure glad colouring of spring flowers which makes us love the Paradise of Fra Angelico.

But if we stand long enough before it a great awe steals over us, and we forget to look for bright colours and gentle angel faces, for the figures surging upwards are very real and human, and the Paradise into which we gaze seems to reveal to our eyes the very place where we ourselves shall stand one day.

At the time when Tintoretto was painting his `Paradiso,' his little daughter Marietta had grown to be a woman, and her painting too had become famous. She was invited to the courts of Germany and Spain to paint the portraits of the King and Emperor, but she refused to leave Venice and her beloved father. Even when she married Mario,

the jeweller, she did not go far from home, and Tintoretto grew every year fonder and prouder of his clever and beautiful daughter. Not only could she paint, but she played and sang most wonderfully, and became a great favourite among the music–loving Venetians.

But this happiness soon came to an end, for Marietta died suddenly in the midst of her happy life.

Nothing could comfort Tintoretto for the loss of his daughter. She was buried in the church of Santa Maria dell' Orto, and there he ordered another place to be prepared that he might be buried at her side. It seemed, indeed, as if he could not live without her, for it was not long before he passed away. The last great stormy picture of `the furious painter' was finished, and all Venice mourned as they laid him to rest beside the daughter he had loved so well.

PAUL VERONESE

It was in the city of Verona that Paul Cagliari, the last of the great painters of the

Venetian school, was born. The name of that old city of the Veneto makes us think at once of moonlight nights and fair Juliet gazing from her balcony as she bids farewell to her dear Romeo. For it was here that the two lovers lived their short lives which ended so sadly.

But Verona has other titles to fame besides being the scene of Shakespeare's story, and one of her proudest boasts is that she gave her name to the great Venetian artist Paolo Veronese, or Paul of Verona, as we would say in English.

There were many artists in Verona when Paolo was a boy. His own father was a sculptor and his uncle a famous painter, so the child was encouraged to begin work early. As soon as he showed that he had a talent for painting, he was sent to his uncle's studio to be taught his first lessons in drawing.

Verona was not very far off from Venice, and Paolo was never tired of listening to the tales told of that beautiful Queen of the Sea. He loved to try and picture her magnificence, her marble palaces overlaid with gold, her richly–dressed nobles, and, above all, the wonder of those pictures which decked her walls. The very names of Giorgione and Titian sounded like magic in his ears. They seemed to open out before him a wonderful new Paradise, where stately men and women clad in the richest robes moved about in a world of glowing colour.

At last the day came when he was to see the city of his dreams, and enter into that magic world of Art. What delight it was to study those pictures hour by hour, and learn the secrets of the great masters. It was the best teaching that heart could desire.

No one in Venice took much notice of the quiet, hard–working young painter, and he worked on steadily by himself for some years. But at last his chance came, and he was commissioned to paint the ceiling of the church of St. Sebastian; and when this was finished Venice recognised his genius, and saw that here was another of her sons whom she must delight to honour.

These great pictures of Veronese were just the kind of work to charm the rich Venetians, those merchant princes who delighted in costly magnificence. Never before had any painter pictured such royal scenes of grandeur. There were banqueting halls with marble balustrades just like their own Venetian palaces. The guests that thronged these halls were courtly gentlemen and high−born ladies arrayed in rich brocades and dazzling jewels. Men− servants and maidservants, costly ornaments and golden dishes were there, everything that heart could desire.

True, there was not much room for religious feeling amid all this grandeur, although the painter would call the pictures by some Bible name and would paint in the figure of our Lord, or the Blessed Virgin, among the gay crowd. But no one stopped to think about religion, and what cared they if the guests at the `Marriage Feast of Cana' were dressed in the rich robes of Venetian nobles, and all was as different as possible from the simple wedding−feast where Christ worked his first miracle.

So the fame of Paolo Veronese grew greater and greater, and he painted more and more gorgeous pictures. But here and there we find a simpler and more charming piece of his work, as when he painted the little St. John with the skin thrown over his bare shoulder and the cross in his hand. He is such a really childlike figure as he stands looking upward and rests his little hand confidingly on the worn and wounded palm of St. Francis, who stands beside him.

Although the Venetian nobles found nothing wanting in the splendid pictures which Veronese painted, the Church at last began to have doubts as to whether they were fit as religious subjects to adorn her walls. The Holy Office considered the question, and Veronese was ordered to appear before the council.

Was it, indeed, fit that court jesters, little negro boys, and even cats and pet dogs should appear in pictures which were to decorate the walls of a church? Veronese answered gravely that it was the effect of the picture that mattered, and that the details need not be thought of. So the complaint was dismissed.

These pictures of Paolo Veronese were really great pieces of decoration, very wonderful in their way, but showing already that Art was sinking lower instead of rising higher.

If the spirits of the old masters could have returned to gaze upon this new work, what would their feelings have been? How the simple Giotto would have shaken his head over this wealth of ornament which meant so little, even while he marvelled at the clever work. How sorrowfully would Fra Angelico have turned away from this perfection of worldly vanity, and sighed to think that the art of painting was no longer a golden chain to link men's souls to Heaven. Even the merry–hearted monk Fra Filippo Lippi would scarce have approved of all this gorgeous company.

Art had indeed shaken off the binding rules of old tradition, and Veronese was free to follow his own magnificent fancy. But who can say if that freedom was indeed a gain? And it is with a sigh that we close the record of Italian Art and turn our eyes, wearied with all its splendour and the glare of the noonday sun, back to the early dawn, when the soul of the painter looked through his pictures, and taught us the simple lesson that work done for the glory of God was greater than that done for the praise of men.

Printed in the United States
122225LV00008BA/51/A